Orion Theophilus Dozier

Foibles of fancy and rhymes of the times

Orion Theophilus Dozier

Foibles of fancy and rhymes of the times

ISBN/EAN: 9783337265083

Printed in Europe, USA, Canada, Australia, Japan

Cover: Foto ©Andreas Hilbeck / pixelio.de

More available books at **www.hansebooks.com**

Orion T. Dozier, M.D.

Foibles of Fancy

AND

Rhymes of the Times,

BY

Orion T. Dozier, M. D.

Ye critics who this book peruse,
  And in it find naught to commend,
Please criticise as you may choose;
  Whate'er you say will not offend.
I'd rather have your worst abuse
  Than milk-and-water words of praise,
And silence would more grieve my muse
  Than all the censure you can raise.

Nor will I bend the suppliant knee
  To plead your pardon in advance;
But if my imperfections be
  By you attacked with spiteful lance,
I'll promise then to write no more,
  Unless to do so I may choose,
And then, of course, in that event,
  I'll hinder not my free-born muse.

BIRMINGHAM, ALA.:
Dispatch Printing Company, Printers and Binders.
1894.

PREFACE.

By way of Preface in presenting this little volume to the public, I will state that I make no pretense or claim to literary or poetic ability. Nor do I expect on the issue of this book "To go to bed and wake to find myself famous." Neither shall I expect wealth and laurel crowns to follow, but intend to continue my vocation at the same old stand and still wear my same old hat.

At the age of thirteen or fourteen years my opportunities for receiving an education were abridged by the breaking out of civil war between the States, which ended my days at school. And, when after four years of war, peace was declared, I, like many other sons of Southern men, found it more imperative to pay court at the offices of mammon than to worship at the shrines of Minerva and the Muses; and as my every day since has been devoted to a struggle for existence, I have had but little time for the pleasures of literary pursuits, and have made but little effort for excellence in composition, but have occasionally written verses for my own pastime or to please some friend, and this collection of my writings is only of such as I have been able to collect since the burning of my scrap-book and manuscripts in the fire, which, two years ago, destroyed my office. The chief incentive for publishing the same is to gratify the wish of my children, who will doubtless ever be my most charitable critics. Regretting sincerely that my offering here is not of a higher standard, and trusting that it may evoke no harsher criticism than it deserves, I will let it go to meet its fate.

THE AUTHOR.

DEDICATION.

To the men whose four years' record of courageous warfare in defense of that freedom, enunciated in the Declaration of Independence, and vouchsafed by the Constitution, and in defense of the eternal principles of caucasian regnancy in a land purchased with the blood of our forefathers; to the men most valiant in deed, most brilliant in exploit, most liberal in sacrifice, most unyielding and uncompromising in their fidelity to their cause —*To the ex-soldiers of the Southern Confederacy*—this volume is dedicated with all the love and fidelity of the

AUTHOR.

INDEX.

HUMOR AND DIALECT.

CAMPAIGN

AND

PATRIOTIC.

"THE STARS AND BARS."

The Stars and Bars.

The stars and bars are fallen
  And will never float again,
But bright on history's pages
  It will live without a stain.

For proudest recollections
  Of battles fought and won,
And glorious deeds of valor
  By Southern patriots done,

Will embalm in sacred memory
  That banner bright and dear,
And sound it down the ages
  As the one without a peer.

'Twas born of stern oppression
  And cradled in the storm,
When retributive justice
  Rose, demanding a reform.

And in the name of liberty,
  'Twas christened in the blood
Of heroes and of patriots
  That flowed in crimson flood.

And thus endeared to freedom
  By every natural tie,

Our hearts were rent with anguish
    When we saw it droop and die.

We held it in affection
    And rejoiced to see it wave,
We loved the men who bore it,
    For they were true and brave.

We loved its holy cause,
    The hopes that it inspired,
We honor every martyr
    Who 'neath its folds expired.

We reverence too the chieftains,
    Each and every separate name,
Who 'neath that star-wreathed banner
    Fought and won their glorious fame.

But supported not by nations
    Who beheld it from afar,
Alone it met the tempest
    On the fiery crest of war.

No nation recognized it,
    No arm was stretched to save,
But the world will ne'er forget it
    As the banner of the brave.

But now that flag has fallen
    And will proudly float no more,
Our soldiers' tents are folded
    And the din of war is o'er.

Our cannon throats are silent,
  The sword is in its sheath,
Our camps are all deserted
  Save the silent camps of death.

No sentinel now on duty
  Doth freedom's watch-words tell,
For liberty was ended
  When that glorious banner fell.

OUR SUNNY LAND AND SOUTHERN DEAD.

Fair sunny land—home of the brave
How wondrous and supremely blest!
Like billows on tempestuous sea,
Emotions rise within my breast,
And surging with a pathos deep,
Sweeps o'er my soul in currents grand,
Whene'er I hear or breathe thy name,
Sweet sunny South, my native land.

What other land 'neath Heaven's dome
By braver men was ever trod?
What other land on earth is known
So lavishly endowed by God?
Where else on earth such valorous deeds,
As by our Southern patriots done,

And where, oh where such women true
As here beneath our Southern sun?

Then wake! oh wake! my muse awake!
A glorious theme my soul inspires;
From blue empyrean heights above
Come warm me with celestial fires.
Attune my tongue to grandeur's strain,
And let my words with genius blaze,
Whilst I the glorious task essay—
Our martyred Southern hosts to praise.

But no, ah no! the plea is vain,
No human tongue in words can frame,
Nor wreathe in thoughts however bright,
The measure of their deathless fame.
But everywhere on earth and sea,
Where'er a patriot's heart shall beat,
The welkin with their praise shall ring,
Till eternity and time shall meet.

And till some nobler muse than mine,
Evoked by greater bard than I,
And aided by a power divine,
From bright supernal realms on high,
Shall grasp the poet's flaming pen
With superhuman force to write,
Be mine the will tho' not the power
Their glorious records to recite.

And yet tho' frail and halt of speech,

An humble chaplet I would weave,
To place upon our soldiers' graves,
And grander task to others leave;
For well I know some noble bard,
Some poet greater far than I,
Shall yet arise and grandly sing,
Of those who sleep, but cannot die.

And till the cycling years of time,
Have into dark oblivion rolled,
All love of home and native land,
Their valorous deeds will still be told;
And yearning youth at mother's knees
Will, in the ages yet to be,
By grand example of their deeds,
Learn how to die for liberty.

Thermopylæ and Marathon
For ages held the captive eye
Of all who looked for honored fields,
Where men had taught us how to die;
But now the gaze of all mankind,
Who seek for glory's proudest shrines,
Turns to Fort Sumpter and Bull Run,
To Gettysburg and Seven Pines.

Alexander and the Cæsars great,
Long held the crown of proudest fame;
But lusterless their crowns appear,
Dimmed in the light of him I name—
Of him who's hand ne'er sought to hold

The sceptre over men yet free,
For now, fame's brightest diadem,
Beams in the crown of Robert Lee.

Joan of Arc, the martial queen,
Led forth her ranks in grand array,
And carved her name on fame's proud fane
By valorous deeds in battle fray,
But grander than her grandest march
Is that by Southern women led,
When marching with Spring garlands bright
To deck the graves of our dead.

And grander than all cenotaphs
That ever hand of human reared;
More brilliant than all banners dear
Than ever on the breeze appeared;
More beautiful than brightest star
That shines in vaulted dome of night
Is that sweet homage beauty yields
To those who fought for home and right.

Nor will they as they come to-day,
With evergreens and brightest blooms,
To decorate with tender care
Our sleeping heroes' silent tombs,
Forget or slight those foemen brave,
Who proved through flame their courage true,
But true to Southern chivalry,
With flowers rare their graves will strew.

And you, ye war-scarred remnant brave,
Who loved the cause our Davis led,
Will ne'er forget sweet Winnie dear
Now that her noble sire is dead.
But every weeping orphan's tear,
And every widow's plaintive plea,
Will wake a warm, responsive chord
In every heart of Camp Hardee.

And in that last great coming morn,
When God shall bid all sleepers rise
From earth and seas to camps on high,
Joined heart and hand beyond the skies,
In armistice of eternal peace,
We'll bivouac amid the stars,
And reverence through eternity,
The stars and stripes and stars and bars.

TAKE BACK THE LIE!

Lines suggested on reading a recent speech by General P——r, Commander-in-Chief of the Grand Army of the Republic, in which he denounced the Southern Flag as the emblem of treason.

Take back the lie, base, craven wretch,
Which thy vile lips have dared to speak ;
Such calumny from thy vile tongue,
But proves that thou art base as weak ;
From coward lips such venom vile,
Can only serve to wake disgust
In hearts of all true, noble men,
Who loathe such vipers of the dust.

Then take it back, thou snarling cur,
Insult not with your lying breath
That ensign of a noble host
Now tenting in their camps of death ;
Nor shouldst thou dare with lying tongue,
To slander men whose dauntless might
Made for that flag a name and place—
The grandest on fame's upmost height.

Thine is the craven coward's course,
Hyena-like that dares to tread,
And with thy foul, polluting breath,
Insults the memory of our dead ;
No faintest ray, nor spark of truth,
Doth to thy lying tongue give pause ;
Else hadst thou not, poor, slimy worm,
Have dared to slander such a cause.

How worse than fool, thou poltroon knave,
To basely lie without a reason—
To let thy lying words imply
That our just cause was one of treason.
The banner that thou darest malign
Shall live through never-ending glory,
Whilst all such hissing toads as thou
Shall be unknown in song or story.

What valiant hero of the blue,
Who faced our warriors in the fray,
But knows that only patriots true,
E'er fought so valiantly as they ;
And knows, too, that no traitor band,
In treason's cause was ever fired
To such sublimely daring deeds
As our Confederate hosts inspired.

Then hush, yea, hush, thy putrid mouth,
Go kill thyself, thy meeds to gain ;
Less sinned had Ananias, when
God numbered him among the slain ;
Nor such a crime since Judas' sin
Hath ever dammed with such just reason,
As that thou laidst upon thy soul
In that foul, lying charge of Treason.

LINES FOR DECORATION DAY.

In duteous love we come again
    With evergreens and brightest blooms,
The purest offerings we can bring,
    To lay upon the hallowed tombs
Of our loved and honored dead,
    Whose deeds, heroic and sublime,
Shall be our country's greatest pride
    Through all the years of endless time.

When Northern despots came to rob
    Our country of her liberty,
They flew to arms in her defense,
    And, shouting loud their battle cry,
Unfurled unto the Southern breeze
    The banner of the triple bars
And rushed to meet the coming foe
    Like heroes at command of Mars.

And on the wide spread battle field,
    Like meeting clouds before the storm,
With banners bright and flashing blades,
    They gathered into battle form,
And, in their fervency of heart,
    Swore by the Heaven's eternal host
That they would never yield their rights
    Till tyrants' blood had paid the cost.

And with their bristling bayonets
    They met the raging battle blast,

And 'mid the sulphurous clouds of smoke,
    With which the field was overcast,
Dealt lightning blows for liberty,
    And poured upon the dusty plain
Their precious life-sustaining blood
    As freely as mid-winter's rain.

But now the storm of war is past
    And freedom's flag lies in the dust;
A mock of peace reigns o'er the land,
    And the most sacred, solemn trust
That patriot hearts have ever known
    Is all that we have now to claim—
'Tis but the ashes of our braves
    And honors of their deathless fame.

But when the muse of history wakes,
    Released from bonds of prejudice,
She will the grandest story tell
    Of valorous deeds and sacrifice
That ever graced the page of fame,
    And glory, bright as Heaven's sun,
Will shed a luster o'er the land
    Of Robert Lee and Washington.

And every nation of the world,
    Where honor's loved and patriots dwell,
Will glorify the martyred dead
    Who 'neath the Southern banner fell;
And bards from every clime will come
    To where their cherished ashes lie,

And, catching inspiration there,
  Will waft their praises to the sky.

And nature's God, who rules above,
  Will bless the tributes which we lay,
With loving hand in tender care,
  Upon the consecrated clay
Which lies upon the mouldering forms
  Of as true and faithful band
As ever praised His holy name
  Or battled for their native land.

And with each year's returning Spring
  We'll come with flowers and deck the sod
Which marks each hero's resting place ;
  And, lifting up our hearts to God,
Plead by the justice of their cause,
  For which their noble lives were given,
That we may meet them then at last,
  All gathered safely into Heaven.

SLANDERERS OF GORDON.

(Written when Gordon was candidate for Governor.)

I can't but feel within me rise
  A deep indignant flame
Whene'er I hear ungrateful tongue

Dare to assail the name
Of him to whom we are endeared
  By every sacred tie,
And him with whom 'twere pleasure yet
  To follow and to die.

For, oh, I loathe, hate and despise
  The poltroon and the knave,
Who, serpent-like, will turn and strike
  The hand once stretched to save.
Oh yes, oh yes, ingratitude,
  Of all man's sins the worst,
If there be deeper hells than hell,
  May it be deepest cursed.

Who but the bribe-bought ruffian,
  And self-ignoble clan,
Would so disgrace our noble State,
  By slandering such a man?
A man whose noble, chivalrous heart
  Ne'er hath a pulsing throb
That does not beat for fellow-man,
  For country and for God.

Go to the hundred battle fields
  Where he has bravely stood,
And where, eight times upon their plains,
  He poured his manly blood,
And ask of those historic grounds,
  Both vale and riverside,
If ever duty called to him
  And he the call denied.

And ask you, too, of those who stood
    Beside him on those fields,
If ever once he turned to foes
    And showed his back or heels.
And ask of those who faced him there,
    Those heroes of the blue,
And let him answer, him who dare,
    To say he was untrue.

Then, when the storm of war had passed
    And all our hopes were riven,
When satraps, with their bayonets
    (May they be cursed of Heaven)
Put alien thieves and scalawags
    To rule and rob our State;
Who was it then who led the van
    To shield us from that fate?

Oh, twas that matchless, God-like man,
    That Christian soldier brave,
That statesman and philanthropist,
    Whom God in goodness gave
To point the way of patriots
    Who seek the prize of fame,
And bless us with the heritage
    Of one bright, spotless name.

Then, hark! ye miscreants and knaves,
    Your lying tongues be stilled,
For ev'ry Southern patriot
    With more than scorn is filled.

And hark ye, too, there is a God
   That's ruling overhead,
And hush, lest, Ananias like,
   That God may strike you dead.

THE DEATH OF CHEATHAM.

The grand old soldier, Cheatham,
   Sat dying in his chair,
And visions of the fitful past
   Came crowding on him there.

He saw once more the legions
   And clans of mustering men,
And heard once more the tumult
   Of war's wild, furious din.

He heard the trump and cannons roar,
   The musket's deadly rattle ;
The saber's clash, the yells and groans
   And rush of men in battle.

He saw the rising clouds of smoke,
   He heard the war steeds neigh,
And sniffed upon the sulphurous breeze
   The distant, deadly fray.

And then he heard the double-quick
  Of troopers hurrying by,
And saw, perchance, his battle flag
  Borne bravely still on high.

And as he seemed to hear and see
  Once more the battle storm,
And felt within his aged veins
  His life blood mounting warm,

There woke within his martial breast
  Once more the kindling flame
That nerves the patriot's heart and hand
  To daring deeds of fame.

His chivalrous soul unyielding, too,
  To sickness and to pain,
Broke forth in that wild dream of death
  To lead his troops again.

"Bring me my horse, my horse," he cried,
  The battle sounding nearer,
"I'm going to the front," he said.
  His wife, oh, who can cheer her.

She caught his now fast drooping head,
  She saw his glazing eye;
He'd gone to join the great command
  Of hosts beyond the sky.

ON THE DEATH OF ADMIRAL SEMMES.

Another gallant chieftain
   Of the grand heroic band,
Who in the cause of freedom
   For our blest Southern land,
Stemmed the tide of battle,
   And won a wide renown,
Has doffed his earthly laurels
   For Heaven's brighter crown.

Too unworthy is my pen
   To eulogize his name,
For "earth's remotest nations"
   Are familiar with his fame.
His grand, heroic deeds
   Upon the rolling sea,
Has made his name immortal
   As that of Robert Lee.

But the waves of old Atlantic,
   As they break upon the shore,
Will chant in loudest praises
   His name forever more;
And the proud, unfettered winds,
   As they sweep from pole to pole,
Will chant in mournful dirges,
   His praises as they roll.

While his bright and faithful sword,
   That could not brook defeat,

2

Lies beneath the waves
  In its silent, safe retreat.
And there 'twill rest forever,
  Without a blot or stain,
The peerless gem of gems
  That decks old Ocean's main.

BRAVE NICKELL OF KENTUCKY.

All through the day in battle fray
  Brave Nickell nobly stood,
And when the fight had closed with night
  And the field was red with blood;
When all had fled except the dead
  Of his followers on the field,
He stood alone with flashing gun
  Disdaining still to yield.

Like lightning's crash his carbine's flash
  Rang out with fearful dread,
And every peal from out his steel
  Still added to the dead.
Loud bursting shell around him fell
  And fast the bullets flew,
But, trusting God, he trode the sod,
  A hero brave and true.

But e'en the best must take their rest,
  And he must sleep at last,
And ere the dawn of coming morn
  The tyrants held him fast.
His arms they bound and round him wound
  Long cords of strength and power,
And Martial Judge, with spiteful grudge,
  Soon fixed his fatal hour.

Yes, right away he fixed the day,
  And in the self-same breath,
With demon smile, named Johnson's isle
  His place to meet his death.
But not a word or muscle stirred
  When the sentence struck his ear,
He stood alone, like cast of stone,
  Unmoved by grief or fear.

And when he stood and calmly viewed
  The beam and dangling rope,
His manly will, with courage still,
  Unblanched by flight of hope,
Showed from his eyes, without disguise,
  A heart with pluck imbued—
A soul of flame, which would not tame,
  Nor be by death subdued.

No friend was there his thoughts to share,
  No priest with him to pray;
But never man, since time began,
  Met death with less dismay.

To friends in gray he bade them say,
  When death had closed his eye,
That true to God and native sod,
  He never feared to die.

JEFF. DAVIS.

With love, almost idolatry,
  I reverence and revere
That grand old Southern patriot
  Who stands without a peer,
The grandest chieftain of the age,
  Tho' clouded by defeat,
The one true heart that never quailed
  Nor bowed at victor's feet.

His was the noblest, truest hand
  That e'er held helm of state,
And tho' by war's wild storms oppressed,
  He bravely met his fate.
Nor prison walls nor victor's chain
  Could e'er his heart subdue,
To will of God alone he bows,
  The truest of the true.

I love him for his constancy,
   And glory in his fame.
Compared with all his enemies,
   He puts their best to shame.
He is the grandest, noblest type,
   Of all our chivalry,
And for himself or Winnie's sake
   "I'd lay me down and die."

THE DEATH OF JEFFERSON DAVIS.

The grand old hero sleeps at last,
   His life's long march is done ;
The grim night watch his post has past
   And left him all alone.
No war's wild note shall wake him more,
   No tyrant's hand shall harm ;
In bivouac of death he sleeps
   Secure from all alarm.

No royal crown e'er pressed his brow,
   Tho' kingliest he of men,
And, tho' in death he slumbers now,
   'Tis not for tongue or pen
To add unto the chaplets green
   Which fame for him has wove ;
A patriot true without a stain—
   A man that gods might love.

His glorious sword, long laid aside,
　　Is rusting in decay;
His noble voice in halls of state
　　Is silenced now for aye;
But history's muse, with flaming pen,
　　When writing Davis's name,
Will leave on time's eternal scroll
　　The brightest gem of fame.

GORDON.

Ye Southern sons of valiant sires,
　　Ye comrades of the knight,
Whose name your country's heart inspires
　　With glory and delight;
Behold him stand before us all,
　　A hero without stain,
Calling us with honest call,
　　And shall he call in vain?

Are we to dumb forgetfulness
　　So quickly fallen prey,
That all his gallant deeds for us
　　Like dreams have passed away?
Did he not for us shed his blood,
　　When souls of men were tried?
And is there anything too good
　　To be to him denied?

No, no! thank God, in Southern breasts
   Ingratitude dwells not;
And he who once our love possessed,
   Shall never be forgot.
Old Shenandoah may cease to roll,
   Virginia's mountains fall;
But Gordon's name on freedom's scroll,
   No time shall e'er appall.

Go mark ye on his martial cheek
   That glorious diadem,
That doth to us more loudly speak
   Than all the tongues of men.
He is our Chevalier Bayard,
   Our more than Marshal Ney;
A patriot praised by every bard,
   "The right-hand man of Lee."

And see upon the minaret
   Of fame's eternal height,
His name and fame in glory set
   To shine forever bright.
Then let us rally round our chief,
   Our leader grand and great,
'Til all his foes are put to grief,
   And he be chief of state.

MOURN, GEORGIA, MOURN.

Mourn Georgia, mourn, my native State,
Sad seems indeed thy bitter fate ;
Thy banner proud that never trailed,
By demagogues is now assailed,
And thy bright star of rising fame,
Seems doomed at last to set in shame.

Thou hast before been sore distressed,
When alien foes thy strength suppressed,
And held thee down 'neath tyrant heel,
Whilst scalawags might rob and steal ;
But tyrant's hate and heels to crush
Could never give thee cause to blush.

Unhappy then as was thy curse,
Thy bitter fate must now be worse—
To feel the shame, to see and know
'Tis thy own sons inflict thy woe ;
That they, who nurtured on thy soil,
Now robber-like would thee despoil.

Hear now that mob in scorn deride
Thy patriots and thy men of pride,
Whom they have dragged with malice vile
From seats which chumps will now defile—
From places high that gave thee fame,
Which now, alas, must bring thee shame.

But hear me; O, fair Georgia, hark!
There yet remains one man of mark,
Who's hand thy honor yet may save.
He is thy patriot—Gordon—brave,
Spurn not his proffer, ere too late
In sackcioth thou shalt mourn thy fate.

CLUB SONG, No. 1.

(Air, Auld Lang Syne.)

Good night! good night! Taps now resound,
  May guardian angels keep
A faithful watch by every couch
  Where comrades fall asleep.

And when, at dawn of rosy morn,
  The birds sing reveille,
Let every Regent don his crown
  Of white supremacy.

Let noble deeds of comrades true
  A shield unto us be,
And true to our just cause and God,
  We'll rule the land and sea.

A PLEA FOR UNITY.

Hear me, sons of Alabama !
   Hear, oh, hear my earnest plea !
Cease thy fratricidal warfare ;
   Our nation's eyes are turned on thee.
Let not demagogues and traitors
   With anarchistic tongues inflame
Thy loyal hearts with madness blind
   To plunge thy State in gulfs of shame.

Let thy pride of race unite thee ;
   Thy birthright in this godly land ;
By God's ordained supremacy
   Thine is the right to still command.
Then spurn, oh, spurn with bitter scorn
   The leadership of selfish knaves
Who fain would foist upon us all
   A rulership of former slaves.

Ye have in times that tried men's souls
   Displayed your valor and your might
And borne through fiercest battle storms
   Old Alabama's banner bright,
And now when threat'ning dangers lurk
   On every hand and every side,
Oh, will ye, worthy patriots,
   Let aught your noble ranks divide ?

Our glorious Southland's holy cause
   A true Caucasian pride inspires

In every heart and honest breast
　Of Alabama's sons and sires;
For come what will of weal or woe,
　Our destiny must be the same;
In unity there's honor still—
　Division means defeat and shame.

Then cursed be he whose selfish soul,
　Groping in its darkened cell,
Would on our State such odium bring—
　A degradation worse than h—l.
For when rape fiends and radicals
　Shall grasp once more the reins of state,
God pity helpless women fair—
　Shield and protect them from their fate.

Then let us all together come—
　United firm in heart and hand—
And swear by God's eternal love
　To shield and save our native land.
Yes, swear by God who made the blood
　Which flows in every white man's veins,
That true to our Caucasian race
　We'll loyal stand while life remains.

THE SOLDIER'S GRAVE.

Hallowed by man and blessed by God,
  Is ever the turf which covers the dead,
But doubly blessed and hallowed the sod
  Which lies o'er the martyred patriot's head.

'Tis there that brightest flowers bloom
  And birds in peace most sweetly sing,
While glory there dispels the gloom
  And death itself doth lose its sting.

'Tis there that purest tears are shed,
  Tears, not of pity, but of love;
For tho' we weep above the dead,
  We know the spirit's with God above.

'Tis there that brightest dews are seen,
  'Tis there that winds most plaintive moan,
'Tis there the moon's soft silvery sheen
  Doth lightly rest o'er Heaven's own.

'Tis there that women love to kneel
  When prayers sincere most fluent flow,
For in their hearts they seem to feel
  That Heaven's gain is our woe.

CLUB SONG, No. 2.

(Air, Bonnie Blue Flag.)

We are a band of patriots,
 United heart and hand,
To shield the honor of our race,
 In this our glorious land.
The blood that flows within our veins
 We never will disgrace
By sharing our heritage
 With earth's ignoble race.

CHORUS.

Then rouse ! arouse !
 Let white men all arouse !
Maintaining white supremacy,
 The cause which we espouse.

By laws divine, the right to rule
 This white man's land we claim,
And true to our Caucasian blood,
 We'll not submit to shame ;
Nor will we e'er in peace submit
 To laws which stultify,
But, in the majesty of right,
 We'll rule this land or die.

CHORUS.

OUR SOLDIERS' GRAVES.

Behold the hosts with solemn tread,
    As on in silence now they move,
Amid the graves where sleep the dead
    Who died for this dear land we love.

'Tis not for pride and vain display,
    That they have sought this hallowed ground,
But love's commands, which they obey,
    To honor those who lie around.

See, every hand a garland bears
    Of evergreens and sweetest blooms,
Bathed with the heart's sincerest tears,
    To decorate our soldiers' tombs.

The task is one sublimely grand,
    And all that martyr ever craves,
Or claims of the survivor's hand—
    A tribute to their silent graves.

No monument of lettered stone,
    However high might be its head,
So much of love can e'er make known,
    As do these tears by beauty shed.

And oh ! what more could patriots ask,
    As they look down from heavenly spheres,
And see performed this grateful task,
    Their graves o'erstrewn with flowers and tears ?

DECORATION DAY.

We come again, and with us bring
The sweetest flowers of early Spring,
To decorate the lonely graves
Of our loved, departed braves.

'Tis duty's call which we obey,
That prompts the tributes which we pay
To those who sleep in death's embrace,
Who died for honor of their race.

And as we deck each holy mound,
We'll humbly kneel upon the ground,
And raise our hearts in prayer to God
To bless our patriots' hallowed sod.

A WISH.

(Written soon after the surrender.)

I long for the day and I pray for the hour
  When the cause of the right o'er the wrong shall
    prevail;
When the South shall have gained the means and the
    power
  To make the foes of her liberties quail.

Yes, I long to hear the cannon's loud peal,
  And to see once more our banners unfurled;
Whilst the rattle of guns and the clashing of steel
  Shall announce our cause still alive to the world.

And I long for more leaders like Jackson and Lee,
  To lead us once more our foemen to meet;
That we by the flash of their sabres may see
  How to follow the course of their broken retreat.

And I long to see die the last vandal in blue,
  And to dance to the notes of his funeral knell;
And I long for a hole in the ground to look through,
  When he joins with all his companions in h—l.

MEMORIAL INVOCATION.

Be pleased, O God ! to bless this day,
And bless the tributes which we lay
  Upon the consecrated graves
Of patriots who wore the gray.

Quick to obey their country's call,
When tyrants threatened to enthrall,
  They rallied to the new-born flag,
Ready in her defense to fall.

For justice and for rights denied,
They met the raging battle's tide,
  Which foemen waged against their land,
And in her cause they nobly died.

For native land they fought and bled,
And better blood was never shed,
  Nor ever shed for better cause,
Than was that of our Southern dead.

Nor ever yet in any land
Was marshaled out a braver band,
  Than those who stood on Southern soil
To battle for their native land.

SONG

AND

SENTIMENT.

ALABAMA

Alabama ! Alabama !
  I am dreaming now of thee,
And I see the trend of thousands
  Coming from beyond the sea,
As they mount upon the billows,
  Steaming through the spray and foam,
Wildly joyous at the prospect
  Of an Alabama home.

And I see within my dreaming
  Visions of the future cast
That shall overwhelm with brilliance
  All the glories of the past ;
For I see the spirit Progress
  Hovering o'er thee with her wand,
At whose lightest touch responding,
  Wonders burst on every hand.

She but touches : armies marching
  Come with axe, with pick and spade,
Felling forests, bridging rivers,
  Delving out the level grade
That shall be for steaming chariots
  A double iron-bounded course,
Where the rushing wheels resounding
  Shake the mountains with their force.

Again she strikes, and cities rising
  Like exhalations from the earth,

Sets the mighty world in wonder
  At their unexpected birth ;
And I hear a hum of factories,
  Blending in a ceaseless roar
Like the sound of ocean billows
  Breaking on a distant shore.

And I see thy mighty mountains
  Torn asunder for their wealth,
And I see thy fountains crowded
  By multitudes in search of health.
And I see thy many rivers
  Opening out into the sea,
Vessels crowded—golden freighted—
  Foreign tribute brought to thee.

She strikes again ; thy vales I see
  Are waving with the golden grain
And fleets within thy harbors wait
  To bear it o'er the watery main.
And I see thy rocky hill-sides
  Purpling with the luscious vine,
And I hear the voice of nations
  Praising Alabama wine. .

But now a brighter scene appearing
  Breaks on my enraptured eye ;
Temples grand and halls of learning
  Spread the land like stars on high,
And from out those halls and temples
  I mark the hosts that come and go—

Poets, statesmen and commanders
    Whose fame shall sets the world aglow.

And now, once more I see that wand
    Lifted high, the land to smite,
And superstition's saints and devils
    Take their everlasting flight.
The wand descends: a shock I feel,
    A mist comes over all I see,
My sleep is broke and all my dream
    Has been of "what is yet to be."

GEORGIA.

Hail, my native Georgia!
    Fair are thy sunny skies,
Thy mountains grand on every hand
    In splendor round me rise;
And down thy fertile valleys fair
    Bright sparkling streamlets flow,
Whilst flowers rare perfume the air
    And set thy hills aglow.

Great Empire of the South,
    Of all thou art the best,
For every toil upon thy soil
    Returns a bounty blest.
Thy every mound and every hill

A wealth of minerals hold,
Which waits but skill, the pick and drill,
  Bright treasures to unfold.

Thy rivers at their source
  Flow forth from beds of gold,
And down the land through valleys grand
  They sweep in billows bold,
And on their waves thy commerce great
  Finds exit to the sea,
And nations all, both great and small,
  Pay tribute unto thee.

Thy sons in war are true and brave,
  In peace their virtues glow ;   .
No traitor's name or coward's shame
  Doth thy proud records show,
But thy bright star on freedom's flag,
  As luminous as at birth,
Will ever shine with light divine
  Whilst freedom dwells on earth.

Thou art a land of happy homes,
  Where peace and pleasure reigns ;
Thy pretty girls, earth's treasure pearls,
  Make famous thy domains.
Thou art indeed supremely blest
  By nature's thousand charms ;
Great mines of wealth and founts of health
  Thou claspest in thine arms.

And thou hast many mountains grand,
 And valleys fair to see,
And Heaven's sun ne'er shone upon
 A fairer land than thee ;
And as thy wandering son returns,
 Resolved no more to roam,
He lifts his song in measures strong
 To praise his native home.

RIZPAH.

"And Rizpah, the daughter of Aiah, took sackcloth and spread it for her upon the rock, from the beginning of the harvest until water dropped upon them out of Heaven, and suffered neither the birds of the air to rest on them by day, nor the beasts of the fields by night." II. Samuel, chapter xxi, verse 10.

On a rugged hill in Gibeon,
 Beyond Jordan's verdant plain,
By the hand of God's avengers,
 Were the sons of Rizpah slain ;
Their forms, denied sepulcher,
 Were cast upon the rock
And left for the wild hyena
 And the ravenous vulture flock.

But a mother's love and sympathy
    Ends not with the doomed one's breath ;
Her devotion and her constancy
    Still increaseth after death.
And Rizpah, with fidelity,
    On the rock her sackcloth spread,
And stood alone in mourning
    To guard her cherished dead.

Throughout the entire season,
    From the harvest till the rain,
Her sleepless eyes unceasingly
    Kept vigil o'er the slain.
The eagle screamed above her,
    Wild hyenas came to prowl,
And her heart was often startled
    By the roaming lion's growl.

But with courage never faltering
    She stood from day to day,
A true, unselfish sentinel
    Against the beasts of prey.
The sunbeams burned upon her,
    She bore the night wind's chill ;
But through day time and through darkness
    She was ever faithful still.

The leopard and the tiger,
    When wandering by the spot,
Beheld her steadfast standing
    And dared to touch her not.

The hungry wolves came round her,
  And the lynx with burning eye,
But daunted by her courage,
  Were made to quail and fly.

And alone upon the rock,
  Unrelieved by any friend,
Her long, dark tresses waving
  And disheveled by the wind,
She kept her faithful vigils
  Till her weeping eyes were red,
Her sole and only solace—
  A communion with the dead.

And all the annals of the world
  Since the morning dawn of time
Affords us no example
  More heroic and sublime
Than of this poor, mourning mother,
  Keeping vigils night and day,
To protect her cherished loved ones
  From the birds and beasts of prey.

CLEOPATRA.

AN IMITATION.

Like the glorious lotus blossoms,
  Drifting on the placid Nile,
My spirit soon on Charon's stream
  Shall swiftly glide from portals vile.
Iris! Charmian! heed me quickly:
  Twine my tresses o'er my brow,
Bring my crown and robe me swiftly,
  Antony awaits me now.

From the throne of realms supernal,
  Where forever he must reign,
Antony, my noble hero,
  Calls me to his arms again.
Robe me as befits my station,
  Scent me with the fragrant balm,
Fill with wine my silver chalice,
  My poor, weary heart to calm.

Over Egypt's plains and deserts
  Cæsar's triumphs shall be vain ;
Antony, to mock his victory,
  With his sword himself hath slain,
And Cleopatra's pride unbending,
  Spurns his captive queen to be—
Nurtured on the throne of freedom,
  Egypt's Queen will e'er be free.

What to me is fame and glory,
   What to me is crown or throne,
Since my glorious lord and lover
   On angel Argus' wings hath flown.
Oh, the thought! I cannot bear it!
   In dreams I hearken to his call,
And, waking, meet not his caresses ;
   My soul is turned to bitter gall.

See how firm and true my courage,
   To my breast I press the asp,
And, remembering thee, my lover,
   Smile upon his deadly clasp.
Swiftly now the subtle poison
   Wends its way through every vein ;
Noble hero, demi Atlas,
   I will soon be thine again.

Though thy wrecked and scattered galleys
   Strew the beach on Actium's shore,
Though thy eagle-crested warriors
   " Bear thy banners high no more ; "
Though thy fame of rising splendor
   O'er the world no more may shine,
Thou hast won a grander victory—
   Cleopatra's heart is thine.

'Twas for thy " Star eyed Egyptian "
   Thou didst fling a world away—
Fame and glory, throne and power,
   Bartered for her love a day.

Thou, the mighty, great triumvir
  Whom great Cæsar feared to meet,
Rome beheld an humble subject
  Suppliant at a woman's feet.

Think not of thy fair Octavia
  Weeping in her widowed home,
For 'twas God our loves united,
  Not the shallow forms of Rome,
And it may be in the future
  Touched by time's soft, soothing art,
That the blow will be forgotten
  And love again revive her heart.

"Though the world for this condemn thee,"
  Thou wert grand to spurn its hate;
God ne'er made thy matchless passion
  But to find in me its mate.
And I, too, can face its frowning,
  Gladly on thy breast to lie,
And, when sable death divides us,
  Gladly for thy love to die.

Let my courage prove my passion
  Whilst the asp now drains my breath,
And, with crown and queenly vesture,
  I dare to follow thee in death.
Haste to meet me at the river,
  Haste! oh, haste! to meet thy bride,
Stretch thine arms and guide me safely
  O'er the dark and chilling tide.

Dim and dark grows all around me,
    Sense and sight are failing fast ;
Never love like mine was fettered—
    Death will make me free at last.
Hark ! I grope in Stygian darkness ;
    Come, fair Iris, bear me home.
Antony, my love, my hero,
    Stretch thine arms, I come ! I come !!

POLICY.

Talk not to me of policy,
    Of what I should or shouldn't do,
For, steadfast to my principles,
    I my course will still pursue.
Let judgment shape my actions
    And my conscience be my guide,
For I'd rather face a frowning world
    Than yield my manly pride.

My religion and my politics
    May I never seek to hide ;
Let me steer with honest purpose
    Though I stem against the tide.
And fettered not by policy,
    By precept nor advice,
I'll bravely meet my destiny,
    Though I plunge a precipice.

No, I will not be a puppet
   To any servile course,
Though bribed by wealth and laurels
   And urged by tyrant force;
But my deep and clear convictions
   Shall ever serve to sway,
And, with conscience for my shield,
   Only God I will obey.

Then away with all your policy,
   'Tis dissembling and deceit—
A smiling lie upon the lip—
   A vain, pretending cheat.
'Tis born of fraud and cowardice,
   No truth is in its name,
And I'd rather lose this heart of mine
   Than sear it with its shame.

Yes, I loathe and scorn the hypocrite,
   Whose life's a living lie;
Who smoothes his actions and his speech
   With the oil of policy,
Who stoops to public favor
   At every bend and nod,
And brings disgrace upon the form
   Made in image of my God.

THE ARMY OF TEMPERANCE.

The banner of temperance now widely unfurled
Gives cheer to the nation and hope to the world.
Its bright gleaming folds lends a glow to the sky,
And thousands have sworn to support it or die;
And whilst the Creator remains on His throne
Its fall or dishonor shall never be known.
Raised by oppression in the cause of the right,
All lovers of justice will 'neath it unite;
For wherever the presence of Bacchus hath been
Grim death and despair are there to be seen;
Men he has murdered by millions untold,
Destroying their souls ere their bodies were cold;
Bright homes he hath plundered of comfort and
     wealth,
Made oceans of tears by destruction to health.
The kind, loving father has changed to a fiend,
The wife from her husband's affections hath weaned,
The love of the husband has changed into strife,
Both blasting the love and the hopes of his wife.
'Twixt brother and brother raised barriers of hate;
The orphan has left unprotected to fate;
The widow and children hath robbed of their bread,
And left them to perish with hunger—unfed.
Great minds hath he robbed of wisdom and reason,
He has bribed the assassin and paid for arch-treason.
In the altars of God he hath found himself place,
And left there the traces of shame and disgrace.
Sweet maidenly virtue hath robbed of its prize,

And done enough sin to have blackened the skies.
Great kingdoms hath conquered, and banners hath
    furled,
And spotted with graveyards the face of the world.
He hath built on the earth the devil a throne,
And consigned those to hell whom Heaven should
    own.
Yes, these are the things which Bacchus hath done,
But soon, thanks to God, his dark course will be run.
Yes, mark me now well, the bright day 's near at hand
When the curse of rum shall be swept from the land ;
Throughout the wide world, from anear and afar,
The armies of temperance are gathering for war.
Justice and virtue, truth, honor and right,
United with temperance have joined in the fight,
And like the swift avalanche gathering in force,
Overleaping obstructions that lie in its course ;
And like the great tides of the ocean in storm,
Uprising in might like mountains in form,
Will come the grand army with banners all bright
To battle for temperance, for God and the right.
No loud booming guns will sound in their wake,
They come not the lives of mortals to take ;
No steel in their hands will be reddened with blood,
No ruins mark places where houses have stood,
No wails from the widowed and orphaned you'll hear,
No red mangled corpse will be seen on its bier,
No tramping of steed or wild clashing of steel
Will be heard when these armies their presence re-
    veal ;

But softly as glides the bright clouds overhead,
And silent as voices which speak from the dead,
Will come this great army, majestic in might,
Bearing down on the wrong, defending the right.
No loud beating drums, nor shrill screaming fife,
Shall jar on the ear, giving token of strife ;
But a calmness like that of a lake in a cave
And a peace undisturbed as the peace of the grave
Shall reign o'er the land, and the country will seem
Like heavenly paradise viewed in a dream.
The army is moving and soon will be here,
Even now in the distance its columns appear,
See, the hovering clouds which have darkened the
      sky,
Recede and give light as the army draws nigh.
Yes, mark you how firmly and grandly doth move
This army approaching with banners of love ;
'Tis coming, victorious, to claim its dominion,
'Tis the army of temperance—Public Opinion.

THE UNFORTUNATE'S PLEA.

———

Though clouds of adversity darken my life,
And the star of my fate goes down in the strife,
Though my destiny yields me but troubles and care,
And my poor aching heart is rent with despair ;
My lips shall be mute to the struggles within,
And the shafts that are hurl'd, in my heart to descend,
Though striking their mark, the wounds I'll conceal,
And bravely repress the anguish I feel.

Though my friends all forsake and the world doth
    condemn,
Though my breast with its sorrow is full to the brim,
Though my hopes are all blasted and my prospects
    are fled,
Thank God for His strength ; my conscience, not dead,
Still glows with its ardor for justice and right,
And my soul still unawed by oppression and might,
Bids a defiance to the wrath that is hurled,
And gives scorn in return for the scorn of the world.

Never my motives have been understood,
Or else they have basely been misconstrued ;
My actions suspected, my kindness abused,
My sympathies spurned, my good will refused ;
The serpent of slander hath traversed my fame,
And his trail so polluting hath sullied my name ;
But the lurements of creed, of power and gold,
I've spurned from my breast like wolves from the fold.

And never will I while on earth I remain
Seek from the world its plaudits to gain,
Nor bow to the shrines of fashion and pride,
Nor steer my course with the popular tide ;
For policy's rule, and bigotry's reign,
Awake in my soul its deepest disdain,
And I turn in my loathing of hate and disgust
From the soulless throngs, so false and unjust.

They boast of religion and love for mankind,
But damning a man for the bent of his mind,
Cry infidel, heretic, knave and fool,
To all who refuse their shackles and rule ;
Dissenters they place on Procrustean bed
And shorten their limb or sever their head,
Or lengthen them out by chains and by screws,
Thus making them gauge to their orthodox views.

Fraud and chicanery in politics rule,
And the greater the knave, the better the tool,
And if he, in fraud, ignore the just laws,
The louder will be the acclaim of applause.
Thus goes the world with popular sway,
Vice is triumphant and justice gives way,
And judges in ermine their benches disgrace,
And the people are taxed to keep them in place.

'Tis ever the same, in state and in church,
When charity's wanted 'tis found in the lurch ;
Religion and freedom exist but in name,
They both have their riders and have a like aim.

'Tis self aggrandizement, wealth, power and fame,
And the means they pursue the devil would shame,
But to be not aboard with the popular tide
Is to have them abuse and your conscience deride.

But why should I sigh or my race execrate
When God is supreme over church and the state,
And sooner or late will His vengeance be hurled,
To right all the wrongs and sins of the world.
Yes, soon or late, with Him must abide
The judgment of all of whatever side;
Then the weak shall go up and the strong shall come
　　　down
And justice shall wear the laurel and crown.

Yes, life is but transient and short at the best,
And beyond the dark grave is the haven of rest;
And there shall my spirit, when its trials are done,
Mount to the throne my conscience hath won,
And receive from my God, for whom I have wrought,
The palms and the crown for the battles I've fought,
And, folding my pinions, forever I'll rest
In the mansions prepared for the weak and oppressed.

NOT FOR BREAD ALONE.

(Response to F. L. Stanton's " Writing for Bread.")

What, tho' you sit and silent write
Amid the still and gloom of night,
Where feebly flickers, faintly falls,
The lamp's dim light on barren walls;
Bend not in melancholy mood,
Nor think of thy surroudinngs rude,
For every care that haunts thee now,
And casts its shadow o'er thy brow,
Shall melt like mists and roll away
And thou shalt see a brighter day.

But think not that you sit alone;
Some glorious muse—all thine own,
Is ever with thee—with her wand
To touch thy pen and guide thy hand
And make thy each and every line
With inspiration's glories shine,
And brightly gild thy every page,
Which, brightening with each coming age,
Shall yield thee more than bread alone—
Undying fame—and sculptured stone.

This world is not an empty dream,
Howe'er deceptive life may seem;
But rich and wide its fields are spread
For those who toil for fame and bread;
And love and tenderness and worth,

Like flowers that spring from mother earth,
Will ever bloom and bud and twine
Around the poet's sacred shrine,
And thy sweet song, in sadness sung,
Shall live when death has stilled thy tongue.

Thy quick'ning breast by misery wrung
Has given the charm to songs you've sung;
For, in thy sad and plaintive strain,
Thou hast but voiced each brother's pain,
Who daily strives for daily bread
And feels, in famined heart unfed,
That subtle longing and unrest
Which all have felt but ne'er expressed;
And while with you our tears we shed,
We'll give you love as well as bread.

Then rouse thee, brother, raise thy head;
Thy path, though not with roses spread,
Is not more rough than all must tread
Who strive and toil to earn their bread.
Alone in labor can be found
The priceless boon of great renown;
Then mourn not that thy genius bright
Must burn apace with lmp at night,
For by its pale and flickering flame
'T will light you on to deathless fame.

And when thy pen is laid to rest—
The pen which oft thy hand has pressed,
(With burning heart and aching head—

And thou art numbered with the dead—)
Thy genius then shall claim its meed,
Thy soul on food of gods shall feed
And thou shalt taste the nectar wine
That gods prepare for souls like thine,
And in Elysian regions blest
Thy soul shall have eternal rest.

THE RATIONALE OF SIN.

(A reply to Rev. Fred. J. Estes' "First Cause of Woe.")

How long shall the fables
  Of mythology last,
Defaming Jehovah
  And his glories o'ercast?
Oh, dark superstition,
  Thou shadow of night,
How long wilt thou linger,
  Man's reason to blight?
How long shall the falsehood
  That a snake of the sod
By men be acknowledged
  As more subtle than God?
How long shall the darkness
  Of ignorance prevail
And the foul tongue of slander
  God's wisdom assail?

Did the great living God,
   Whose hands did create
This world we inhabit,
   And ten thousand more great,
Whose will is but nature,
   Supreme of all law,
And whose mind from the first
   All the future foresaw,
Make man pure and holy—
   From sin pure and bright—
And ordain that no sin
   Should his prospects e'er blight;
Then make a vile serpent
   And into him instill
The vile power to break
   And defy His own will?

Oh, believe it not so—
   'Tis false and untrue—
For God, the all-wise,
   Would not such folly do.
Yea, God is all wisdom,
   And when He made man
He made him, no doubt,
   On a rational plan.
He endowed him with sense,
   With conscience and might,
And made him free agent,
   To do wrong or do right;
For without the extremes

Of evil and good,
How could he serve God
As really he should?

Had there never been sin
From which to abstain,
All conscience and reason
Were but attributes vain;
And my conscience and reason,
Inherent from birth,
I would not surrender
For all fables of earth.
And I'll tell you just here,
As I have told you before,
To God, in our wisdom,
We should bow and adore.
Then never, oh never,
Defame thy great God
By making Him less
Than a worm of the sod.

To thee He gave conscience,
A heart and a brain,
And thou shouldst not bury
Thy talents in vain.
Look around, look aloft,
Let your reason be free;
Behold His great works
On the land and the sea;
See mountains and rivers,

Volcanoes and seas,
Great oceans and lakes
  And forests of trees;
Then list to the thunder
  And the lightning's wild crash;
Hear the roar from the shore
  Where the tempest waves dash;

Then turn thy gaze upward
  To the great arching sky
And view thousands of worlds
  That bedazzle the eye—
Each rolling in splendor
  Through infinite space,
Each controlled in their movements
  Or held in their place
By the hands of the great God,
  Whose will they obey,
And whose power and greatness
  Can never decay.
Then reflect, if you will,
  And believe, if you can,
That this great supreme God
  Ever formed Him a plan

And had not the will
  And the power to make
That plan all secure
  From the lies of a snake.

COOSA RIVER.

A REVERIE.

Roll on, oh gentle Coosa,
   Thou art dearer far to me
Than all the other waters
   That flow into the sea.
From thy early fountain source,
   'Mid the Georgia mountains grand,
Down through old Alabama
   To the ocean's pearly strand,
Thou art peerless in thy beauty,
   Thou art ever fair and bright,
And everywhere I view thee
   There is gladness in the sight.

What memories, sweet and tender,
   Of my by-gone happy days,
Now fills my heart with rapture
   Whene'er on thee I gaze.
Those happy days of boyhood,
   That can bless me never more,
Were spent with boon companions
   In sporting on thy shore ;
And, oh, what royal pleasure
   'Twas to plunge into thy tide
And, like the wild aquatic birds,
   On thy placid bosom glide.

Ah, well do I remember
    One blissful summer night,
When moon and stars of Heaven
    Made thy crystal waters bright,
Of floating down thy current,
    Borne onward by the tide,
In sweetest little shallop,
    With fair Inez by my side ;
When I told her of my love,
    As I clasped her to my breast,
And, in answer to my wooing,
    Heard her love for me confessed.

Then again upon thy borders
    On a lovely day in May,
With flowers blooming 'round us
    And the birds all singing gay,
How I led off in the dance,
    With a merry, happy train,
Whirling in a giddy waltz
    With blithesome Kitty Dane,
The fairest little fairy,
    To my bosom firmly pressed,
And felt her heart responding
    To the throbbing in my breast.

There 'neath the beech and maples
    That shade thy grassy shore,
Near the village of Coloma,
    In the halcyon days of yore,

Where I was want to wander
　　To view thy lovely sheen,
Hand in hand with pretty Lizzie,
　　The little village queen,
And with her there to angle,
　　With our hooks oft baited not,
All forgetful of the fishing,
　　So contented with our lot.

Then drifting, gently drifting,
　　Adown thy placid stream,
Borne onward to Aurora
　　In my retrospective dream,
I meet once more the loved ones,
　　Both my friends and kindred dear,
And view once more the prospect
　　That was wont my heart to cheer,
And see once more around me
　　Those winsome girls and boys
Which made that village on thy shore
　　The Eden of my joys.

But roll on, noble river,
　　My retrospect is vain,
Whilst thou shalt flow forever,
　　I shall never feel again
The rapture and the ecstacy,
　　And charms without alloy,
That blest me in those sunny days
　　When I was yet a boy,

Sporting on thy bosom,
  Or romping on thy shore,
With precious friends and loved ones,
  In those happy days of yore.

MAN WAS MADE FOR WOE.

Go search the world from pole to pole,
  And view mankind in every state;
You'll never find a living soul—
  What'er his land, what'er his fate—
Who has not felt within his breast
  The tides of sorrow ebb and flow,
And has not felt, when care oppress 'd,
  That mortal man was made for woe.

The loving swain in lonely bower
  In fondness burns with passion's flame;
Each budding bloom and blushing flower
  Reminds him of his cherished dame.
But, when a few short years have fled
  His youthful cheek has lost its glow,
In tears of disappointment shed,
  He learns that man was made for woe.

And he, the pampered man of pride,
  With hoarded wealth of precious ore,

With teeming acres, broad and wide,
  Who daily scorns the weak and poor,
Will, when his frame with age is bent,
  And every step 's a painful throe,
In his cold heart his pride repent,
  And murmur, "man was made for woe."

The royal king and lord of state,
  Flushed with men's homage and with fame,
May for a while forget that fate
  Has made all human kind the same;
But, ere for them life's sun shall sink,
  A Marah's draught for them must flow,
And, as they quaff the bitter drink,
  Must learn that man was made for woe.

Vain is the Bacchanalian cup,
  And vain is worldly wealth and fame;
The cup of sorrow all must sup,
  In differing phase, but all the same.
For some must burn 'neath Tropic sun,
  Some perish in the Arctic snow,
And some have treasures, some have none,
  But all must have some bitter woe.

Such is the destiny of man,
  And it is just as we shall find,
A part of the Creator's plan
  To teach us to be good and kind,
To succour those who need our care,

And to withhold each cruel blow;
For, as a brother's care we share
So shall we lessen our own woe.

CUPID'S AUCTION.

Behold upon the market stand
    A lovely gem of radiance rare,
With which no pearl of Eastern land
    In point of beauty can compare;
'Tis brighter than a diamond far,
    More lovely than the fairest star,
More precious than Arabian gold,
    It's worth in words can ne'er be told.

It hath no duplicate on earth,
    And heaven claims no fairer gem
Of perfect cast and peerless worth
    Than this endearing diadem;
But here it is, and to be sold,
    For highest price, to young or old,
'Tis true no small bid will suffice;
    Then let us hear the highest price.

Deceitful Flattery, first to speak,
    Now makes an offering fraught with pride,
He compliments the glowing cheek,
    With raven curls on either side;

5

Then adds unto with tenderness
    A praise of form and style of dress,
And seeks by bid of coxcombs' art
    To gain the prize unto his heart.

Then Beauty, clothed with faultless style,
    Made offering of his handsome face,
O'er which there played a sunny smile,
    And bowed with an artistic grace,
Which seemed to say in language plain,
    He had no doubt the prize he'd gain ;
He doubtless thought his face and form
    Would take the precious gem by storm.

Next pompous wealth's defiant voice
    Proclaimed a bid of indolence,
And added gifts of Mammon's choice
    In part, by way of recompense,
And with base heart and haughty pride
    Thought other bids to set aside ;
For gold hath such a charming touch,
    Naught else, he thought, availed so much.

Then intellect, with modest grace,
    Announced his bid—a wealth of mind,
And by the beam upon his face,
    He deemed the prize for him destined ;
For who, with privilege to choose,
    Could such a bid as his refuse ;
His wit and wisdon, so well known,
    He thought would make the gem his own.

But Love, all friendless and alone,
  At once upon the scene appears,
And prays to make his offering known ;
  A bid it is of sighs and tears—
A yearning of a constant heart,
  Whose constancy would ne'er depart,
A manly soul, unknown to fear,
  A faithful arm to do and dare.

A mind in which daily nurture
  Sweet visions of the gem herself,
Feet which know but paths of virtue,
  Hands clean of all dishonest pelf ;
All these the bid which Love would give ;
  Now tell me, shall his bidding thrive ?
Oh, if ! oh, if ! you answer yes,
  Long will I Cupid's auction bless.

A HUNTER'S WISH.

My former home and friends I've left,
  And sought the forest's rugged wild,
Whose primeval grandeur as yet
  The hand of man hath not defiled ;
And though it is 'mid scenes like these
  That I have always loved to dwell—
And tho' there's much to please me here,
  I still have cares I can't dispel.

For when upon the mountain's top
  I stand with rapt, enchanted gaze,
On lovely scenes which meet my view,
  Bathed in the distant mellow haze,
Within my heart, so lone and sad,
  I feel a restless, longing care,
For one on whom my soul is set
  Is not with me the scene to share.

And when beside the flowing stream,
  To Undine's song I bend my ear,
And lightly tread the mossy bank,
  The sweet, low murmuring song to hear ;
'Tis then I feel how sad it is
  To waste upon the listless air
So much of nature's melody,
  And she not here the song to share.

And when engaged in flying chase,
  Excitement thrills my panting breast,

And climbing up the mountain's side,
  I pause awhile to watch and rest,
And see the stag and hounds go by,
  As if in flight of wild despair,
There comes, amid my wildest thoughts,
  A wish that she the scene might share.

And when the sable shades of night
  Have fallen over hills and plains,
Whilst tired nature takes its rest,
  And deep, unbroken silence reigns,
'Tis then, in gloominess of mind,
  I think of her so bright and fair,
And from my heart there steals a wish
  That she my loneliness might share.

A WOMAN OF THE TOWN.

Only a fallen woman,
  Mark the paint upon her cheek,
That hides the faltering blushes
  Where modesty would speak ;
Spurn her from your church's door,
  Seat her not in sacred pew,
Her soul is steeped in vileness,
  Let her learn her wrongs to rue.

Bar all your homes against her
   And spurn her on the street,
Let her ears to scornful hisses
   Hearken when you chance to meet.
She has parted with her virtue,
   She was tempted and she fell,
And now, with scornful daggers,
   Help to drive her on to hell.

Jesus, the dying saviour,
   Only shed his precious blood
To pave the way to Heaven
   For the virtuous and the good.
The unfortunates of passion,
   And of man's deceiving lies,
Must never hope for pardon
   Nor to mount the christian's skies.

If she ask of you for bread,
   Be sure you give her a stone—
Perhaps 'twill gall her conscience
   And extort a deeper groan.
Let her feel your pious vengeance,
   Crush her heart beneath your heel,
And think how Christ will bless you
   For the spirit you reveal.

Never touch her sinful hand,
   Nor beside her kneel and pray ;
Shut the book of life against her,
   Let her go her sinful way.

Sting her with contumely,
  Never let to her be known
That Christ said that the sinless
  Should be first to cast a stone.

Oh, you hollow-hearted men,
  And you women in your pride,
Behold this fallen outcast
  While your consciences decide
If you should have forgiveness
  For all your sinful stains,
While she, poor erring mortal,
  Must, unpitied, wear her chains.

THE WRECK.

'Tis over now, the dream is past,
A dream it was—too bright to last;
I know the worst, I feel it all,
  My last bright hope has fled;
I take the cup and drink the gall,
  Though tears no more I'll shed.

Yet, welling up in memory strong,
I measure still the awful wrong;
His loving words were, oh, so dear,
  I blindly followed on,

And now there's naught my heart to cheer,
  My faith in man is gone.

But oh, unequal and unjust,
That he who won my love and trust,
And then betrayed me to my shame,
  Tho' guiltier far than I,
Escapes the penalties and blame,
  Whilst I must more than die.

For I have learned, alas, too late!
To mourn my sad and bitter fate;
Have learned in bitter anguish deep
  How base man is—unjust,
And learned how useless 'tis to weep,
  When conquered by his lust.

But so it is, the die is cast,
The past is now forever past;
Nor pleading prayer, nor mints of gold,
  Nor all my curses vain
Can lift the guilt from off my soul,
  Nor bring my virtue back again.

Could I alone but bear the shame,
And sully not my parents' name,
My bleeding heart should bleed alone,
  My lips should murmur not,
And I might stifle every groan,
  And cease to wail my lot.

But when I think that with my fall
My friends, my brothers, sisters, all,
And every kindred link on earth
    Must share the blighting shame—
Indeed, my babe before its birth—
    The thought doth wreck my brain!

Ah, yes, ah, yes, e'en now I feel
My vague and wandering senses reel;
Black demons strike and serpents dart,
    And fiends, the blackest, round me yell;
My friends forsake, my heart strings part;
    Oh, welcome death and hell.

MY FRIEND.

My friend of to-day is my friend of to-morrow,
His joy is my joy, his sorrow my sorrow;
Let him be what he will, his acts I approve,
For I see not his faults, so great is my love.

I've known him full long and know him full well,
And his many good traits 'tis useless to tell;
But sufficient to me is this above all,
He's a friend unto those whom misfortunes befall.

He wears not the symbols of creed or of church,
But when charity calls is not found in the lurch,
And bearing no trumpet to sound his own praise,
His conscience by him is more treasured than bays.

Never daunted by fear, when dangers arise,
Nor wearing a mask, his thoughts to disguise:
He's a friend to his friends and a foe to his foes,
And his actions his noble impulses disclose.

He is rich, but not rich with silver and gold,
Nor many broad acres hath he to control,
But richer, far richer, than Crœsus, the king,
His wealth is the peace his conscience doth bring.

Unsordid, unselfish; he's a man I can trust,
For his words and his deeds are all meant to be just,
And though he may err in whole or in part,
'Tis a fault of his judgment and not of his heart.

And now, as in future, "let fate do her worst,"
My hopes be destroyed, my prospects accursed;
Come weal or come woe, let me sink or swim,
I'll be true to my friend though the world should
        condemn.

And were there some ruby or diamond, more bright
Than the fairest of gems in the crown of the night,
And should all the stars turn to diamonds and fall,
I would not give my friend, if I could, for them all.

TO-MORROW.

To-morrow, to-morrow,
  Alas, for poor me!
I've been waiting so long
  The morrow to see
That would bring me surcease
  From sorrow and care,
And ease my poor heart
  Of the pain that is there.

But, oh, the to-morrow
  For which I have sighed,
I fear will ne'er come
  'Till the fountains are dried
That now give a vent
  To my anguish and woe,
For my only nepenthe
  Is when my tears flow.

All the friendship I've known
  Was sordid and base,
All the love I have sought
  Was a butterfly chase;
When the prize I had seized,
  The attraction had fled,
And my poor, hungry heart
  Left in hunger unfed.

All the hopes of my youth,
  My castles in air,

Built for the morrow,
  So brilliant and fair,
Have moulded in ruins—
  Have gone to decay,
And to-morrow so bright
  Is still far away.

The dream of to-morrow—
  How false was the dream—
That to-morrow would come
  With a bright, sunny beam,
Dispelling the shadows
  That darken my life,
And light up my soul,
  Now gloomy with strife.

Yes, false was the dream,
  Each day is the same,
The morning but dawns
  To rekindle the flame.
Of longing for pleasures
  I never can know,
Then turns into darkness
  And leaves me in woe.

But to-morrow will come,
  Oh, welcome the day,
When my heart shall be still
  Beneath the cold clay;
My pulseless, pale hands
  Across my cold breast,
My soul with its God,
  My body at rest.

THE RIGHT.

To my son Byron.

On the world's broad stage of action,
  Whatsoever part you play,
Let it be your soul's attraction
  To do all the good you may ;
Heed you not the voice of jeering,
  Notice not the foes who slight ;
Lift your head with manly bearing,
  Let your motto be " The Right."

Seeming friends will round you linger,
  When your labors meet success,
But will point a scorning finger
  When they see you in distress ;
And it may be they will trample
  On you with a tyrant's might,
But forbear from their example,
  Let your motto be " The Right."

Oft temptations in your pathway,
  Like fair roses will be spread ;
Deceitful charms to lead astray,
  Hiding dangers from your tread ;
For oft beneath " fair roses " lie
  Serpents of most deadly bite ;
So always keep an open eye,
  Let your motto be " The Right."

First see that what you undertake
  Is just and right before you start,
And when you've done so, loose the brake,
  Then push ahead with all your heart;
Think not of troubles on the track,
  Tho' many dangers meet your sight,
Face them and bravely force them back;
  Let your motto be "The Right,"

Should slanderers your name assail,
  Turn away with heedless ear;
Should friends forsake and fortune fail,
  Still to duty persevere;
For every star that shines above
  Shines brightest on the coldest night;
So let the stars a lesson prove—
  Let your motto be "The Right."

And when from earth you pass away,
  And your soul on wings of love
Has reached the shores of endless day
  In the spirit land above,
You'll find inscribed above the throne,
  In characters of living light,
The motto which has been thine own—
  The golden motto of "The Right."

GIVE ME FOR A FRIEND.

Give me for a friend
    The warm hearted man,
Who dares to do right,
    Whatever betide ;
Whose love-beaming eye
    Some virtue will scan
In the worst of all those
    Whom braggarts deride.

I ask not his name,
    Nor care for his birth ;
Whether Gentile or Jew,
    No need to inquire ;
Whether highly in fame,
    Or lowly of earth,
If his heart warmly beats
    With love-kindled fire.

Yes, give me the man
    Whose soul-beaming eye
Grows moist with a tear
    At pity's appeal,
And who to the call
    Is ready to fly,
And a liberal heart
    By actions reveal.

Yes, give me the man
    With carriage erect,

In the lines of whose lips
　　True courage I'll trace ;
Who's slow in a friend
　　A fault to detect,
But ready and quick
　　A foeman to face.

Let him be a true man,
　　From dogmas all freed,
Whose mind is his book,
　　His conscience his guide ;
Who deigns not to stoop
　　To priest-ridden creed,
But walks by the light
　　Which God has supplied.

GOOD-BYE.

An Evening Reverie.

Impelled by that resistless fate,
　　Which guides me with an iron hand,
I must forsake the scenes of late,
　　To roam again some other land.

For it has ever been my lot
　　'Mid strangers all my life to roam,

And never find on earth a spot
  That I may even claim as home.

And knowing not where next I'll be,
  I follow on without a fear,
For since these scenes no more I'll see,
  There's nothing else excites a care.

But let me go where e'er I may,
  There's not a scene that I'll forget;
There's not a friend but every day
  I'll think of with a sad regret.

*Nebo and Hebron oft' will rise
  In sweet imaginative view,
And, looking on the starry skies,
  My soul will all its hopes renew.

*Round Island, too, and Bethlehem
  Will in affection ever dwell,
For sacred truths first learned in them
  Have sunk in memory's deepest cell.

And friendly faces that I've loved,
  Imprinted on my inmost heart,
Will linger there by time unmoved,
  And only with my life depart.

There's Robert L——, my noble friend,
  From whom I part with keenest pain,
For him my love shall never end,
  Tho' we may never meet again.

Yes, and there is still another—
  Dear Thomas S—, whose generous heart
Makes me love him like a brother,
  And grieves my soul that we must part.

And oft' when I in slumbers lie,
  My soul, escaping from my breast,
Will back to Minnie swiftly fly,
  And vigils keep while she's at rest.

But why should I their names repeat,
  Or let my muse their virtues tell,
When we on earth no more will meet,
  So, friends and loved ones, fare ye well.

*Nebro, Hebron, Round Island and Bethlehem were names of
churches in ——— county, Ala.

WAITING AND DREAMING.

I am waiting, I am dreaming,
  While the years are rolling by,
And my hairs are whiter turning,
  And a dimness of my eye
Is the all that I am gaining
  From the swiftly passing years,
Save the shortening of my journey
  To the bright celestial spheres.

All my labors now are ended,
  Every task is finished now,
For the stamp of many winters
  Is imprinted on my brow;
And a·dreaming now I ponder,
  While the years are flitting by,
Yes, I'm dreaming of the pleasures
  Of a home beyond the sky.

Of life's years I've had full measure,
  And I've borne my load of care;
I have tasted earthly pleasures,
  And of troubles had my share;
Now I'm growing old and feeble,
  And my journey soon will cease,
For by day and night I'm dreaming
  Of sweet heaven and its peace.

Many friends have gone before me,
  Whom I long once more to see;
Many loved ones, too, are waiting
  There to greet and welcome me;
And while waiting and a-dreaming,
  As the years are rolling by,
I can almost hear their voices
  Chanting anthems in the sky.

In my Savior I have trusted;
  He has given me the peace
That the understanding passeth,

And my longing doth increase
There to stand within His presence,
And be known as I am known ;
And awaiting I am dreaming
Of sweet Jesus and His throne.

I'M IN LOVE WITH TWO GIRLS.

I'm in love with two girls—
Now isn't that queer—
One's a little brunette,
The other's quite fair ;
They both are so pretty,
So sweet and so dear,
To say which is dearest
I can't, I declare.

But of this I'm assured—
They dearly love me ;
Are not the least jealous
Wherever I be ;
I know they are constant
And true in their love,
And ne'er will forsake me
Where ever I rove.

There are others, I know,
More sweet—debonair,

But in my affection
  There's none to compare
With these little ladies
  Of whom I'm so fond—
My black-eyed brunette
  And rosy-cheek blonde.

I said that I loved them,
  But feebly expressed
How deeply abiding
  Their place in my breast ;
And the wealth of a world,
  In diamonds and pearls,
I would count as but dross
  Compared to my girls.

And there is another,
  Of whom I've not told,
And with whom I'm in love,
  Tho' now she is old,
She's the queen of my soul,
  The charm of my life—
My little girls' mama,
  My own precious wife.

DYING ABELARD.

Here within this gloomy abbey,
    Where I came to hide my shame,
I now welcome death's approaches
    Which must soon my spirit claim.
Years have passed since first I entered,
    Through this ill-foreboding door,
Casting off the wreaths of laurel,
    Which in glory once I wore.

And with memories wrought in sorrow,
    Slowly wearing out my life,
I have prayed the coming summons
    That should end my bosom's strife.
And now as the sable shadows
    Darken o'er my glazing eye,
Calmly I receive the warning,
    Feeling that 'tis sweet to die.

But oh, my faithful Heloise,
    To thee my dying spirit flies,
And the past with sorrows laden,
    In my burning thoughts arise;
And I see thee pure and lovely,
    As before I brought thee shame,
And I hear thy earnest pleading,
    To forsake thee—for my fame.

And I see the look of anguish
  Settle on thy features still,
As when first the curse of passion
  Triumphed o'er thy virtuous will.
O, the memories of that hour;
  How they cling with keen regret,
Would to God my awful sinning,
  I could banish or forget.

All my fortune, fame and glory,
  I relinquished for thy smile,
Smothered was my soul and conscience,
  By my passion's subtle guile,
And when all too late repenting,
  I had taken thee, to wife,
Fulbert, in his brutal vengeance,
  Worse than robbed me of my life.

Hark, methinks I hear thy voice,
  Yes, O yes, I see thy face;
Quick, my long neglected idol,
  Clasp me in thy warm embrace;
Lay thy hands upon my brow,
  Whilst those burning lips of thine
Impart once more their latent heat
  To these freezing lips of mine.

Alas! 'tis o'er, 'twas but a dream
  Of my rack'd and frenzied brain,
And thou—my own sweet Heloise,
  I will never see again.

Still and dark is all around me,
    Soon my breast will cease to swell,
God of mercy shield and keep thee,
    Sweet Heloise, fare thee well.

WAITING AND LONGING.

How long seem the days, and what ages the weeks,
Since, darling, my lips I last presssed to thy cheeks ;
And oh ! with what longing, what anguish and pain,
I wait for the day when I'll see thee again.

The nights are so long, so lonely without thee,
My thoughts and my dreams are ever about thee ;
Sleep woos not my lids, tho' tired and weary,
Life is a burden, existence is dreary.

In bright gilded halls of pleasure's resort,
Where the joyous and gay with companions consort,
The laughter there heard and all that I see,
O'erwhelms me with sadness and longings for thee.

On the streets when I stroll and join in the throng
Of multitudes rushing, hurrying along,
All aimless I wander on no mission bent,
And naught that I find can bring me content.

O, what in this life is worth living for me
When thy face and thy form no longer I see,
No music can soothe me, no pleasures delight,
When thou art not near me my life is a blight.

Then fly ye winged hours and hasten the day
That shall bring me surcease from my longing dis-
  may;
When the sunshine of love, the smiles of my wife
Shall banish the darkness that shadows my life.

A LOVER'S PIQUE.

Fair girl, if thou could'st only know
 How much of love thou art possessed,
Thou would'st the cruel slights forego
 By which my heart's so oft distressed;
Nor would thy lip, in cold disdain,
 E'er with scornful smile reprove me,
Unless 'tis pleasure to give pain
 To one who cannot help but love thee.

Nor would that sparkling eye of thine
 E'er blanch me with its glance of hate,
Nor would'st thou scorn these tears of mine,
 And bid me curse my bitter fate.
Nay, nay, not so, if thou but knew
 How helpless I am to control

The flame of love which lit by you,
　That day and night consumes my soul.

But pity would with soothing wand
　Thy heart to soft impulses move,
And thou who art so proud and grand,
　Would'st pity my unhappy love ;
Repentance, too, within thy heart,
　Would'st fill thy lovely eyes with tears,
And bid thy quivering lips impart
　Sweet words of solace to mine ears.

But go ! thy pity I disdain.
　My manhood's pride is now returning,
For tho' I've loved so long in vain,
　The flame at last must cease its burning.
Yes, true, for even whilst I write,
　Altho' the change has come so late,
My soul's aglow with new-born light,
　From fires of newly kindled hate.

Yes, go ! and be thou cursed or blest,
　Thy love and pity I disdain,
For now I feel within my breast
　No more the slightest touch of pain,
Nor would I lose one single breath
　To yield a sigh of one regret,
But rather would I face my death
　Than suppliant sue to base coquette.

THE EXILE'S WISH.

When my summons of death shall come,
   And I must lay me down and die,
I wish to be afar from home
   Where not a single weeping eye
Shall look upon my pallid brow
   And mark the heaving of my breast,
For were my senses then as now,
   I could not calmly sink to rest.

Nor do I wish in that dread hour
   The sobs of grieving friends to hear,
And know that 'tis not in my power
   The sadness from their hearts to cheer;
Nor would I feel upon my cheek
   The tender touch of loving hand,
Nor list to lips which faltering speak
   The glories of a better land.

But rather in some lonely cave,
   To all the world but me unknown,
Be mine, the exile's unsought grave,
   Where, soothed by the ocean's moan,
Without a tear, without a groan
   To end this troubled life of mine
And leave my dust, my mouldering bones,
   Where sun or star-rays never shine.

WOMAN AND THE SNAKE.

Reply to Rev. F. J. Estes.

I hold it true
And still maintain
This fact where e'er I go;
That I or you,
What e'er we do
Are heirs to pain and woe.

Old mother Eve,
The apple ate,
From the forbidden tree,
And I believe
'Twas to conceive,
And so caused you and me.

We all are here
How e'er it be,
And all must multiply,
And all must bear
Pain, grief and care,
And in the end must die.

God willed it so,
We can't deny,
Or else it ne'er had been;
And so 'tis so
That all our woe
Is not produced by sin.

In Eden fair,
Ere man was made,
Jehovah's will was law ;
The tempter's snare
And man's despair
God doubtless all foresaw.

And had he not
Ordained that Eve
Should of the apple eat,
Old Eve, I wot,
Had never got
Deceived by such a cheat

And when you try
The fact to screen,
God's word you must forsake,
For all must die,
Both she and I,
Said God ; not so the snake.

And death, you see,
Brings pain and woe ;
And troubles multiply,
And you and me
And all we see,
Must suffer, toil and die.

And good or bad,
'Tis all the same,

We can't amend the law;
 And whether glad,
 Or whether mad,
It ain't no use to jaw.

AN EVENING REVERIE.

The sinking sun's last lingering light,
 Has tinged the Western sky with gold,
And deepening shades of coming night
 Now gathering round me I behold.

The sweet refreshing evening breeze
 About my brow begins to play,
And now I see through yonder trees,
 Bright Jupiter's first twinkling ray.

And while I sit in calm repose,
 Recalling memories of the past;
Long by-gone days again disclose
 Sweet scenes of youth too bright to last.

Sweet home, dear place of peace and love,
 Hallowed by a mother's tread;
To thee in thought I swiftly move,
 And greet the loved ones that are dead.

Then off again in fancy's flight,
  To school—the place of youthful joy—
Where merry faces greet my sight,
  Whom once I loved when yet a boy.

Then on the tented field of Mars,
  Through battle smoke with rallying cry
Beneath the glorious "stars and bars",
  I strike for Southern liberty.

Next with the throttle in my hand,
  My throbbing locomotive flies
From town to town—across the land,
  Like meteor across the skies.

Then sitting down by Eula's side
  I clasp her little hand in mine;
And while the moments swiftly glide,
  I drink the nectar—love divine.

Such are the scenes that swiftly pass
  Before my fancy in its range,
Made dim by "memory's mellowing glass",
  And proving time's eternal change.

But folded be my fancy's wings,
  That bear me back to scenes of gladness,
For now each scene my bosom wrings
  With keenest pangs of grief and sadness.

Indulging in a boyish freak—
  A wish in other lands to roam,

Now makes my heart grow faint and weak,
   When e'er I breathe the name of home.

The schoolmates of my boyhood's day,
   From all save memory have fled,
While many of my friends in gray,
   In camps of death their tents have spread.

And she for whom I would have died,
   False to her every vow has proved,
And with the scorn of wounded pride
   I cursed the day I ever loved.

But there is one with noble heart
   Who faithfully to me has stood,
And of my cares hath borne a part,
   When spurned by those of nearer blood.

Yes, noble girl—my Ossie dear,
   What, though I search the world around,
A heart more true, a face more fair
   Than thine, sweet girl, can ne'er be found.

And while my heart beats warm and free.
   Whatever skies above me bend,
Remember, dear, you have in me,
   A cousin and a faithful friend.

NATALITIA.

Written before marriage to my wife on the occasion of her 16th birthday.

Just sixteen years have passed away
   Since precious Lizzie's natal day ;
Just sixteen years since Nature's God
   Looked down from His abode above
Upon this dreary mundane sod
   And saw it had no queen of love.

Then, to an angel by his side
   He did the task of love confide
To search through all the hosts of heaven
   And find the brightest seraph there,
That she might to the earth be given,
   As reigning queen of all the fair.

The angel then, with that command,
   Flew round among the angel band,
And, searching, found—a fairy sprite,
   With raven curls and snowy breast,
And rosy cheeks and eyes of light,
   Which brighter shown than all the rest.

And as no fairer could be found ;
   Around that sprite her arms she wound,
And, spreading forth her wings of white,
  . Flew swiftly down and brought to earth
That little queen—the fairy sprite,
   And gave to her terrestrial birth.

7

And since to earth this queen was born,
  The ranks of beauty to adorn,
With every year more fair she's grown,
  'Till I have vowed that little elf
Shall rule but one, and one alone,
  And I shall be that one myself.

THE CRIMINAL'S COMPLAINT.

The king of day on radiant car
  Now mounts up in the eastern sky,
But ere his daily course be done,
  The sleep of death shall close my eye.

Tried by a jury and condemned,
  The haughty judge my sentence read,
Which dooms that I this day shall hang
  By my neck 'til I am dead.

But is it just, or is it right,
  That I should yield this life of mine
To atone for an unconscious act,
  Done when my mind was crazed with wine?

And is it either fair, or just,
  That he who poisoned me with drink
Should go unpunished by the law,
  Whilst I must by its sentence sink?

For had he robbed me not of mind,
　By giving me the liquid fire,
I never would have done the crime
　For which I must this day expire.

Then is he less than I to blame
　In that dark deed of bloody strife,
Which makes two loving mothers mourn,
　And makes a widow of my wife?

No, Heaven's court will grant it not,　·
　Tho' courts of men may so proclaim,
And in the final judgment day
　He'll not escape an equal blame.

Then be my curse upon his head,
　Until he feels what I have felt,
And on him rest my victim's blood,
　Who fell beneath the blow I dealt.

*SOUTH ROME.

South Rome, superb, thy mountains grand
Around thee like great sentinels stand,
   To keep and shield thee from alarm,
   When storms arise and threaten harm;
And from their grand, majestic domes
Look down on smiling, peaceful homes;
   Whilst gushing fountains, pure and bright,
   Break from thy hills, and in the light
Of sunbeams sparkling, ever sweet,
Forever cool, doth lave thy feet
   And yield a glow to every cheek
   For those who come, sweet health to seek.
But not alone thy lovely mountains,
Crystal streams and sparkling fountains;
   These are not half the splendid charms
   Which thou claspest in thine arms;
But fairer far than Sharon's fields,
And all the wealth Golconda yields;
   More precious, too, than all the wine
   That e'er was brewed from luscious vine;
Yea, fairer far than India's pearls
Thy greatest charm—thy pretty girls.
   God bless them, each and every one,
   No fairer dwell beneath the sun;
Then be thy boast thy daughters fair,
Whose loveliness and beauty rare

Beggars the power of pen to tell,
Each one's a queen—a reigning belle,
A sweet enchantress be it said,
Whose footsteps bless the land they tread.

*Rome, Ga.

---

*WAITING AT THE RIVER.

"Lord, how long shall I have to wait
  Before I cross the river?"*
I long to reach that other shore,
  Where I can rest forever.

My journey, Lord, has been so long,
  Life's wilderness so dreary;
My burden's been so hard to bear;
  My soul is faint and weary.

Then haste, oh, Lord, to speak the word,
  And bid my waiting cease,
I fain would leave this dreary shore,
  And reach the land of peace.

Whilst here I wait, oh, Lord, I bear
  Most grievous griefs and pain,
My weary soul now turns to thee,
  And pleads that land to gain.

'Tis dark and chilly on this shore,
   But over the stream I see
The sun still shining warm and bright,
   Where loved ones wait for me.

My heart, oh, Lord, has long been there,
   With all I love the best;
Oh, send thy angels, precious Lord,
   And lead me to my rest.

My father's face I long to see,
   My saintly mother's, too,
And many children gone before,
   Oh, Lord, are there with you.

Do, precious Saviour, haste to speak,
   And bid me now to come,
And join the bright celestial band
   In my eternal home.

* Almost the last words of my aged father, Rev. Dr. T. H.
Dozier, while on his dying bed, were: "Oh, Lord, how long shall
I have to wait before I cross the river?"

GOOD-BYE SONG TO F. L. STANTON.

Good-bye, good-bye, dear friend, good-bye,
　　God's blessings on thee we implore,
And speak with a sigh, our parting good-bye,
　　As you leave to meet us no more.

Our joys and cares with us you 've shared
　　Revealing a friendship sincere,
And now as we part, the grief in each heart
　　Is shown in a shimmering tear.

Within our minds we'll ever keep
　　Your memory, so precious and dear,
And time cannot change or ever estrange
　　The love you have won from us here.

Henceforth, afar from us you go,
　　Your duteous paths to pursue,
But oft in our eyes bright tears will arise
　　As we think of your last " adieu ".

And now, good-bye, a last good-bye,
　　Our hearts with sweetest sympathies swell,
Our spirits grow weak, our lips fail to speak—
　　Dear friend and companion, farewell.

DOUBLE ACROSTIC.

On every hill and mountain's height,
   Down in earth's dark and shady caves,
Roaming o'er sandy deserts white,
   On the broad ocean's dashing waves,
In the bright starry realm above
   Reigns supreme, the God of love.

On the sweet voice of flowing rills,
   Amid the roar of rushing tides,
Nature's faint echoes from her hills,
   Sighing in winds that ne'er abides,
Descending with the falling rain,
   The voice of love is ever plain.

On pale Luna's face at night,
   Upon the azure milky way,
Zone bound in Saturn's mellowed light,
   Beaming in the Sun's bright ray,
In beams of Mars and Mercury,
   Beautiful in Venus' purity.

Exquisite in Jupiter's bright glow,
   Shining Uranus and Neptune too,
   Reveal to us of love, a view.

SHALL I FORGET?

Shall I forget sweet Dora's face?
  A face so dear in days gone by,
Shall I forget her winsome grace,
  The brilliance of her jet black eye?
No, whilst my memory keeps its throne,
  I'll curse the day when first we met,
And though my heart's as cold as stone,
  Her beauty I can ne'er forget.

From land to land, from sea to sea,
  I've fled without an aim in view,
But like a dream, where e'er I flee,
  Her haunting face my steps pursue;
Her words of scorn and cold disdain
  Within my heart are rankling yet,
And though I struggle, 'tis in vain,
  Her lovely face I'll ne'er forget.

But I will not attach a blame,
  To one of such transcendent charms;
For heaven itself would blush with shame
  To see such beauty in my arms.
'Twas fate that taught my youthful heart,
  Its love upon such charms to set,
But fate can never teach the art
  To change from love and then forget.

Then marvel not that on my brow
　The clouds of grief and sorrow rest,
For love can make the strongest bow,
　When that love remains unblest;
Yes, darker than the shades of hell,
　Is love that lingers in regret,
No light can e'er its gloom dispel;
　It never, never can forget.

LOVE'S PLEA.

When lips to lips, and breast to breast
In tenderness of love are presssed,
There speaks a voice from out the heart,
That faltering words can ne'er impart;
And love's sweet music through the voice,
Makes all within the soul rejoice.

And thus it ever is with me,
That when thy rosy lips I see,
Or mark the heaving of your breast,
By virtue and by beauty blest,
I long to clasp thy heart to mine
And kiss those wooing lips of thine.

But now, alas! too well I know,
That such vain thoughts I must forego;
Such thoughts I never should have known—
But nature's thoughts are not my own;
And, while each grace you may retain,
To banish thee, I try in vain.

LINES TO LULA.

For three long years of toil and strife,
    But one impulse has filled my breast;
One single aim has been my life
    An only hope my heart hath blest.

And should I now that impulse name,
    Or speak the aim my life hath held,
Alas! 'twould be but to proclaim
    That impulse, aim and hope dispelled.

For thee on whom I gazed with pride,
    To whom I gave my constant heart,
Hath all thy love to me denied
    And bid me from thy thoughts depart.

With coldness thou hast spurned my love
    And wrung my heart with grief and pain,
But it may be that time will prove
    What thou hast lost by thy disdain.

COULD I THE MUSES' AID BUT CLAIM.

Could I the muses' aid but claim
　　To wake my soul's neglected lyre,
And thus unveil the hidden flame
　　Of my heart's consuming fire.

I would on fancy's golden wing,
　　Soar to some realm with visions fraught,
And swift returning, with me bring
　　From that bright isle the gems of thought.

And then with glowing words to chime
　　Sweet Lula's worth I'd panegyrize,
That she in mirrowed thoughts sublime,
　　Might view herself in glad surprise.

And paint I would, in hues divine,
　　The glory of her winsome face,
That those who should its light define
　　Would worship its Madonna grace.

And then, with inspiration's touch,
　　I'd paint in wreathing glories fair
The sweet, sweet smile I love so much,
　　That some bright angel's kiss left there.

Then of each flaming, living page,
　　Sparkling with the muses' lore,
" Penned by poet and by sage,"
　　None than mine could please her more.

TO MINNIE.

Tho' thy bright smiling face but twice I have met,
Its impressions with me I can never forget.
It will cling to my mind wherever I be,
And keep me, dear girl, ever thinking of thee.

When flying by steam o'er the smooth iron rail,
Or cleaving the wave neath the white spreading sail,
Wherever I roam, on land or the sea,
I'll be thinking, dear girl, be thinking of thee.

When I view the great mountains eternal with snow,
Or traverse dark caverns, earth's surface below,
'Mid whatever scenes, wherever I flee,
I'll be thinking, dear girl, be thinking of thee.

When lightly I trip in the merry quadrille,
Or fly in the chase over valley and hill,
'Mid every gay thought, in the height of my glee,
I'll be thinking, dear girl, be thinking of thee.

Should fortune e'er bless me and fill from her store
My purse and my coffers with bright shining ore,
As I count o'er the mass, each piece that I see,
I'll be thinking, dear girl, be thinking of thee.

But should fate, in a mood, some spite to appease,
Lay my form low with some destroying disease,
I'll smile in defiance of her saddest decree,
And be happy, dear girl, by thinking of thee.

And when all my labors on earth shall be done,
And I view the dark shadows of life's setting sun,
Like an angel beside me, thy face I will see,
And be thinking, dear girl, be thinking of thee.

LINES FOR AN ALBUM.

Dear Carrie!   In thy happy days
    When thy hopes and prospects blend,
When flattery speaks profuse thy praise,
    Let me be to thee a friend.

And when thou art vexed in mind
    And thy hopes with fears contend,
Whene'er thou would'st solace find
    Let me be to thee a friend.

When seeming friends deceive thy trust
    And thy loving heart doth rend
When all the world's to thee unjust,
    Let me be to thee a friend.

When care hath settled on thy heart
    And life its joys doth suspend,
And when from thee thy hopes depart
    Let me be to thee a friend.

When after death thy spirit free
  Doth to realms of light ascend,
I'd have thee then remember me,
  Thy truest, dearest, earthly friend.

LIFE.

The dew which comes with stars of night
To glisten in the morning's light,
An hour sparkles on the grass,
And then doth into vapor pass.

And flowers which in morning bloom
And lade the air with sweet perfume,
Live not to see the close of day,
They lose their charms and pass away.

The bright rainbow which spans the sky
An arch of gold it seems on high,
A moment lingers to our view
And then bids us a slow adieu.

The snow which falls with beauteous flake
Upon the bosom of the lake,
Quick disappears and leaves no trace
Of its eternal resting place.

And these are all mere types of life
In this dark world of toil and strife,
One day we're born, the next we die,
And then within the dust we lie.

But oh, how sweet to feel and know
That death is but an end of woe,
That tho' we die upon this earth,
Our souls will have a happier birth.

'TIS THEN I THINK OF YOU.

When mock-birds chant their matin lay,
  And the sky's roseate hue,
Proclaims the dawning of the day,
  'Tis then—'tis then I think of you.

And when at noontide's sultry hour
  The sky is one ethereal blue.
And I have sought my shady bower,
  'Tis then—'tis then I think of you.

When night its starry robes reveal,
  And Heaven sheds its glist'ning dew,
When silence o'er the world doth steal;
  'Tis then—'tis then I think of you.

And when in sleep I chance to dream,
  And dream there's naught to cheer my view,
Then, waking, see the moon's bright beam,
  'Tis then—'tis then I think of you.

And thus my joy in life shall be,
  Whilst memory's chain holds firm and true;
Altho' thy face no more I see,
  To sweetly—sweetly think of you.

LINES WRITTEN ON THE FLY LEAF OF
A BOOK.

To her whose curls of ebon hue
   Droop o'er shoulders white as snow,
And from whose eyes, like morning dew,
   Light's brightest scintillations glow.

Whose lovely cheeks are soft and fair
   As ever claimed a poet's thought ;
Whose mind is free from every care,
   Whose soul's with every virtue fraught.

Whose lovely lips, divinely sweet,
   Are worthy of an angel's kiss,
And in whose heart such virtues meet
   As fit her for Heaven's courts of bliss.

Whose form of grace outvies the swan,
   That swims upon the glassy stream,
And whose sweet thoughts from dawn to dawn
   Are bright and pure as angel's dream.

MY LIFE IS LIKE A SHIP AT SEA.

My life is like a ship at sea,
 That wrestles with the storm in vain,
Which only mounts one rising swell
 To be cast down in gulfs again.

My life is like a ship at sea,
 With compass lost and shivered mast;
Tossed here and there upon the waves.
 A wreck that tells of tempests past.

My life is like a ship at sea,
 A lonely barque without a sail,
Deserted by unfriendly crew,
 And left to perish in the gale.

My life is like a ship at sea,
 Which madly stems the driving blast,
But far away from friendly port,
 Is doomed to fail and sink at last.

My life is like a ship at sea,
 That soon will sink beneath the wave,
And, sinking, leave no sign or trace
 Of its eternal resting grave.

LINES SENT WITH A BOUQUET TO LULA C.

Go! ye sweet and gentle flowers,
　To her, your queen, more fair than ye,
And speak with thy celestial powers,
　And bid her kindly think of me.

With your fair charms entrance her eyes,
　And bless her with your sweet perfume;
And when in dreaming sleep she lies,
　Keep silent vigils in her room.

And if by dreams disturbed in mind
　In whispers she should speak of me,
Send back your spirits on the wind
　And tell me what her dreamings be.

And, oh, what rapture 'twill impart,
　If she but softly breathe my name;
'Twill cheer my poor, despairing heart,
　And soothe my love's consuming flame.

Yes, go, fair messengers of love,
　And speak with all thy emblems true;
With fragrant charms her heart assure
　That I my sacred vows renew.

And if she but interpret right
　The message that thy emblems tell,
'Twill make her gentle eyes grow bright.
　And all her cruel doubts dispel.

TO ———.

Dear M———. we have parted forever,
 And the bonds which once bound me to thee
My duty has bid me to sever,
 And to cast them forever from me.

No more thy hand will I press—
 Never more thy lips will I kiss;
Thy form I no more will caress,
 For now 't were unhallowed bliss.

Thy heart no longer mine own—
 Of thy love no more can I boast,
For it to another has flown,
 And from me forever is lost.

But the loss I cannot regret,
 Since thy bliss is a pleasure to me ;
And much joy may thy new love beget,
 I'll rejoice in the pleasure with thee.

When thy lover shall stand by thy side,
 And hold thee close clasped to his breast,
And call thee his own loving bride,
 I will pray that thy loves may be blessed.

THERE IS NO GOD.

The fool hath said there is no God
   But how should that fool know,
Unless all space he had explored,
   In nature high and low;
For if there be one spot or space
   Unknown in worlds or air,
He cannot prove there is no God,
   For may be God is there.

To know, indeed, there is no God
   All force that fool must know,
The power that sends the cyclones forth,
   And hurls the lightning's blow;
For all that he or I can tell,
   Or whence they had their source,
Amounts to nothing but a guess,
   And God may be that force.

Then if he knows all space and force,
   Himself a God must be,
For none but one omnipotent
   Could so much know or see;
And he, indeed, is but a fool,
   Who this great truth denies,
That there is one great living God,
   For nature proves he lies.

INVOCATION.

Thy aid, oh God, to break the spell,
   To lift the veil which shrouds the breast ,
That grieving hearts may speak and tell
   The throes by which they are distressed.

Oh, touch thou, with thy loving hand,
   " The weeping lyre of the heart,"
And bid our souls with love expand
   For him who from us did depart.

Oh, grant Thou light unto our minds
   To sing the worth of one so brave,
Whose soul too pure for earth's confines,
   Escaped to heaven through the grave.

Renew, oh God, our faith in Thee ;
   Inspire our souls with sacred love,
So that, when death shall set us free,
   We'll meet the missing one above.

COULD I FORGET?

Could I forget, could I forget
　　One fair false face that haunts me still,
My last few days of waning life
　　Might find some joy my heart to thrill;
And fondly dreaming, as of yore,
　　On scenes of bliss by love made blest,
I'd calmly drift adown life's stream
　　Till death's oblivion gave me rest.

But, ah, poor me! while life shall last,
　　While thought and memory keeps its throne,
No fond, sweet dream, no wistful hope,
　　Within my breast shall e'er be known;
For disappointment and despair,
　　That came to me long years ago,
Have stamped an impress on my heart,
　　And filled my soul with bitter woe.

And now to me it matters not
　　What course on earth my steps pursue;
No friends I seek, no foes I shun,
　　But knowing death is sure and true,
I bear my lot as best I may,
　　And, longing, wait for that sweet day,
When life shall flutter from my breast,
　　And death's oblivion brings me rest.

BEACHTIFUL ROME.

In a beautiful vale,
    Where the rivers unite,
Surrounded by mountains,
    Majestic in height,
Where old Alto, superb,
    Looks down from his dome,
Is the fairest of cities—
    Our beautiful Rome.

A queen of the valley,
    She lifts her fair head
To view the rich treasures
    That round her are spread,
And invites all the world,
    In search of a home,
To come and be welcome
    In beautiful Rome.

In her arms are embraced
    Great mountains of wealth,
And from her fair bosom
    Flow fountains of health ;
Whilst two rushing rivers
    Lave her feet with their foam,
And ever sing praises
    To beautiful Rome.

With her fair, queenly charms
    She attracts the world's eyes ;

With each move of her hand
　She awakes a surprise,
For she has but to touch
　Her rich valleys of loam,
And their riches fill up
　The coffers of Rome.

Yea, she has but to speak,
　Or to touch with her wand,
And railroads spring forth
　From her magical hand;
Whilst factory and furnace
　Unite with a hum
To swell the grand chorus
　Of beautiful Rome.

THE BALLOT.

On which side are you, my brother?
　'Tis your ballot that will tell,
And will count for you in Heaven,
　Or against you deep in Hell.

Are you on the side of morals,
　Of temperance and the right?
Or are you for the traffic
　Your poor fellow-men to blight?

Are you on the side of Jesus,
  With a love for fellow-man,
Or helping on his ruin,
  By your aid to whisky's clan ?

Are you with the weak and helpless,
  Whom sorrow doth impress ?
Or do you, by your ballot,
  Still sanction their distress ?

Are you on the side of safety
  For the mother, child and wife ?
Or are you for the hellish drink.
  That causes want and strife ?

Are you for the pure and moral,
  Who delight in doing good ?
Or for whisky, rum and riot—
  For tears and sighs and blood ?

Are you for the church and Bible,
  And God's sweet, holy will ?
Or are you for the wicked laws
  That license men to kill ?

Can you vote the drunkard's ticket ?
  Then, on bended knees, at night
Ask God to bless your ballot,
  And to keep your vote in sight.

That in the awful judgment day,
    When called before His throne
To receive your final sentence,
    "You may reap as you have sown."

On which side are you, my brother?
    Will you pause awhile and think,
Ere you slight your God and mercy
    For the devil's fatal drink?

Whatever be your answer
    Your vote will surely tell,
And will count for you in Heaven,
    Or 'gainst you deep in Hell.

Yes, God will read the ballots,
    Each and every one that's cast;
And those that glorify Him not
    The soul will help to blast.

SOME DAY.

Some day, I know, but know not when,
  My pulsing heart will cease to beat,
My weary hands will cease their toil ;
  The quick step of my hurrying feet
Will no more echo in my home,
  Nor loved ones list to hear me come.

Some day, I know, but know not when,
  The sombre hearse will reach my door,
And friends with muffled tread will come,
  Whom I, alas! shall see no more,
And bear me off unto my tomb,
  And leave me there in silent gloom.

Some day my loved ones, left behind,
  Will come to where in death I sleep,
And, placing flowers upon my grave,
  Will linger there awhile to weep—
And breathe for me a silent prayer,
  But I shall never know them there.

Some day, I know, oh, sad the thought !
  My friends and loved ones, too, will be
All cold and pulseless in their tombs,
  And none on earth remembering me
Will ever speak or hear my name,
  For I must die unknown to fame.

Some day the stone that marks my grave,
  That tells my date of death and birth
Will, too, have crumbled into dust,
  And not a vestige here on earth
Will then be left to tell the tale
  That e'er I crossed life's troubled vale.

But far beyond each trembling star,
  Now twinkling in the Heavenly dome,
My soul, released from earthly woes,
  Shall mount to my eternal home,
Where I shall join the Heavenly choir,
  And sing the praise of my Messiah.

NO COMPROMISE FOR ME.

Talk not to me of compromise,
  I loathe, I hate the very word.
It is the strongest arm of him
  By whom the fires of hell are stirred.
Old Satan never smiles so bright,
  Nor darker gloams the frowning skies,
Than when men split the right in twain
  And call that action "compromise."

What, tho' my cause shall ne'er prevail
  I still can bravely bear defeat,
A victor's crown I'd scorn to wear
  If I must stoop that crown to greet;

No, let me live and let me die
  In conscious practice of the right,
My soul unsullied by my vote,
  No act of mine a home shall blight.

Whate'er is right, must right remain,
  Whate'er is wrong must still so be,
No policy for sake of gain
  Can make the right with wrong agree.
Then be your license high or low,
  Your whisky dens are still the same,
Like whited sepulchres without,
  Within there's naught but death and shame.

Tho' dastard dotards humbly bow,
  And bend the weak, the suppliant knee,
Tho' coward cravens cry for peace,
  And talk to me of policy;
I yield to nothing short of truth,
  No sort of compromise I take;
I dare to stand up for the right,
  Tho' cravens all the right forsake.

And as for me and for my house,
  Tho' ballot-beaten still we stand,
Unmoved, unchanged, unconquered still,
  With love for God and fellow-man,
Resolved our purpose ne'er to yield,
  Nor cease to work, nor cease to fight,
'Till gloriously we've won the field
  For God, for justice and for right.

LINES TO J. L. T.

O, tell me not this lovely world
 Is all made up of vain deceit;
That love is all a fickle charm,
 And friendship's nothing but a cheat.

Nor tell me, yet, that man was made
 For naught but labor and for strife;
That he's deception, in himself,
 And there's no constancy in life.

But rather tell me if you will
 That this strong body hath no soul,
And that the God who made the world
 Hath not, above it all, control.

But speak not thus in idle jest,
 No words like these can I believe,
Whilst I can boast one faithful friend
 Who'd rather perish than deceive

A noble, generous friend, is he,
 With ready hand for every task;
For anything, at any time,
 To give, or do, what I may ask.

No sordid craven heart he bears,
 But best impulses fill his breast;
And when I've needed most a friend,
 He's always stood the firmest test.

He's generous, too, to every fault,
  And brave as ever armed knight;
Disdaining all the world might say,
  Content to do what's just and right.

And modest as he's good and brave,
  He seeks not vain and empty show;
But scorns alike the flattering tongue
  And dangers of a skulking foe.

Then tell me not that life's a myth,
  That sincere friendship is unknown;
For one such friend, as Johnnie is,
  To live for, is enough alone.

TO LIZZIE.

Thy pretty face,
Thy lovely grace,
And all thy winsome charms,
With cunning art
Allures my heart,
And all my hope alarms.

Thy lovely smiles,
Thy playful wiles,
And thy coquettish airs,
Entrance my eyes,
Awake my sighs,
And fill my breast with cares.

Thy silvery voice,
Thy words so choice,
When ringing out in songs,
Breaks on my ear,
So sweetly, dear,
My heart their joy prolongs.

THE MURDERED WIFE.

A poor woman, the mother of a young babe, died in Rome several days ago, and her father testified that her death was the result of a beating at the hands of her drunken husband.

Behold, ye "anti-prohi's,"
  Your work is well begun ;
A murdered mother's blood
  Now stains the cause you won.

A helpless little infant,
  In piteous hunger cries,
Whilst its mother's bloody form
  In yonder graveyard lies.

'Twas a husband in his frenzy,
  By whisky driven wild,
Who struck that mother down—
  Made an orphan of his child.

And on you, my "anti" friends,
  Who voted "for the sale,"
Must rest the awful crime
  When justice shall prevail.

For at the Bar of Judgment,
  When God shall call your name,
You'll not escape his vengeance,
  For to you belongs the blame.

'Twas the sanction of your ballot
　　That licensed men to sell,
And the selling brought about
　　That bloody deed of hell.

And that poor murdered mother,
　　At the bar beyond the sky,
Will be a witness 'gainst you
　　When you are called to die.

BE CAREFUL HOW YOU TREAD.

In walking through earth's verdant fields,
　　Be careful where you tread,
Don't crush the little flowers
　　While gazing overhead.
The stars I know are brighter far
　　Than flowers that deck the sod,
But both the flowers and the stars
　　Are handiworks of God.

And in the fields of human life,
　　Oft found in humble ways,
The pure in heart, the mild and good
　　Escape our upward gaze,
And in our rush and wild pusuit
　　Of best in social skies,
We sometimes crush a noble heart
　　That Heaven itself would prize.

INFELICE.

I sometimes wake in the night time,
  And visions come crowding my brain,
Which burden my soul with sadness,
  And which I resist but in vain.
The path of my life's long journey
  A trail through a desert appears,
Where the thorns, the thistles and stones
  Are bathed with my blood and my tears.

All along are the wrecks and the ruins
  Of my prospects gone to decay,
Of idols I loved and cherished,
  All broken and left by the way.
But then, through my tear-dimmed vision,
  That path trending upward I see,
To a home of pleasure and rest
  Where loved ones are waiting for me.

So gathering my remnants of faith,
  And hugging them close to my breast,
As beggars draw closer their rags,
  When by cold and hunger oppressed.
I look no longer behind me,
  But my gaze still upward I bend,
Heedless of what I encounter,
  Resolved to push on to the end.

MY MOTHER'S HEART.

'Tis sweet to feel, what e'er betide,
When friends forsake and foes deride,
That one warm heart beats for me still ;
One heart, which only death can chill.

When somber gloom and cares oppress,
And bitter griefs my soul distress,
'Tis solace sweet to feel and know
That faithful heart still shares my woe.

It matters not what fate be mine,
What star of destiny may shine,
Give fate her mood to frown or smile,
From me that heart naught can beguile.

For when grief's bitter cup I've quaffed,
And writhed beneath a sland'rous shaft,
Or by ingratitude been stung,
That heart to me hath fondly clung.

And when upon a bed of pain
Consuming fevers burned my brain,
And death came near—oh, hideous thing—
That heart was then my sheltering wing.

And now what e'er be fate's decree
Of good or bad in store for me,
I reck not, but let come what will,
Since that fond heart is constant still.

And when I've done at last with earth,
Where claimed by sorrow since my birth,
I hope to see Heaven's portals part
And rest once more on mother's heart.

TIME.

Roll on, roll on, eternál time!
   All nature bows to thee,
The mountains and the hills sublime,
   The rivers and the sea
Shall mingle in one common wreck,
   And earth shall pass away,
Ere thou thy wasting course shall check,
   Or thy destructions stay.

Coeval with the God-head born,
   Coeval with his reïgn,
All human fame thou laugh'st to scorn,
   All monuments disdain;
Thou see'st nations rise and fall,
   And empires cease to be;
O'er burned out world's thou spread'st a pall
   Of darkness like to thee.

Go, puerile man, nor deign to boast
  Thy strength or high estate ;
Suns, moons and stars in darkness lost
  By time's ordaining fate,
Shall leave a black and empty void,
  Where once they bright revolved ;
And all that is shall be destroyed,
  Ere time shall be dissolved.

FAITH.

Beyond the golden sunset
  Of life's departing day
I see a star ascending
  With ever brightening ray ;
Transcendent in its beauty,
  For Faith has made it known,
The beacon of my maker
  To lead me to His throne.

And, arching o'er the heavens,
  The bow of peace I see,
And in it read the promise
  Which God has made to me ;
For I have had the deluge
  Of sin's repentant tears
And I rest upon Moriah,
  Where the cross of Christ appears.

I DO NOT KNOW.

Sometimes I pause in awful doubt
  That God e'er answers prayer,
And ask, if so, why my poor heart
  Is left to its despair;
And why, if God can hear and aid
  The plea of those distressed,
There comes no peace to break the gloom
  That burdens my poor breast.
For earnestly I've sought in vain,
  Through prayer's most fluent flow,
But why my pleas are answered not,
  I do not know, I do not know.

And when I sink into the tomb,
  Shall I yet rise again?
Shall sentient soul rebel with earth
  And breaking death's cold chain,
Leave cold, corrupting clay behind
  And mount to other spheres;
Or sleep in apathetic dust
  Through time's eternal years,
Forgetful and forgot of earth
  With all its joys and woe?
Alas, though oft I question thus,
  I do not know, I do not know.

Beneath my own fair sunny skies,
  Beyond my native land,

'Neath alien stars, in lands afar,
   Beyond old ocean's strand,
I've sought to learn what might be known
   Of God's most holy plan,
To purge the world of wickedness
   And save the souls of man ;
But priests and preachers prate of creeds
   No light can they bestow,
And still in darkness, I confess,
   I do not know, I do not know.

A DREAM THAT WAS NOT A DREAM.

Beside my sweet darling's grave in the city of the
   dead,
I sat until the sinking sun's last ray of light had fled ;
And all alone, I heeded not the ebbing of the day,
For my heart was in the grave, and my thoughts
   were far away.

One by one, the little stars came forth, twinkling
   overhead,
Until the whole of heaven was with beauty over-
   spread ;
The moon, then like a silver ship, came mounting up
   above,
And floated gently onward, as if moved by hands of
   love.

Bright flowers, blooming round me, lent a sweetness
to the air,
But I heeded not their fragrance, nor noticed they
were there;
And there beside the grave, where silence reigned
supreme,
O'ercome at last by weeping, I slept and had a
dream.

I saw the heavens part—heard a sound of thunder
loud,
Then saw descending earthward a shining silver
cloud;
And reclining on that cloud, with bright angels by
her side,
I recognized my darling, my sweet angelic bride.

And as the cloud came slowly down, such music filled
my ears
As I never, never heard before upon this vale of
tears;
And when it came to where I was, it seemed there to
divide,
And my sweet, angelic darling left sitting by my
side.

Around her forehead twined a wreath of softest glowing light,
And the raiment that she wore was a robe of spot-
less white;
Halo's of radiant light all round about us shone,

And the music of her voice was like the Zithern's
    sweetest tone.

She told me of a place above, a happy spirit land,
Where everything is beautiful, majestical and grand;
Where the God of nature sits on a glory beaming
    throne,
Where life is life eternal, and where sorrow is un-
    known.

She told me of friends and kindred all dwelling
    there above,
And from each she brought a message to remind me
    of their love;
Then bidding me good-bye, said she'd wait me on
    the shore
Of that bright land celestial where there's parting
    never more.

Then on that cloud I saw her take a gentle upward
    flight,
And watching 'till she reached the sky, she vanished
    from my sight,
And tho' I knew 't was all a dream, a delusion of the
    brain,
I cannot yet help wishing she may come in dreams
    again.

A SIGH FOR THE SEA.

Oh, give me a home by the deep, blue sea,
   The ocean all boundless and wide,
Let me list to the sounds that ever resound
   In its every sweet, murmuring tide ;
Let me wake at morn, its breakers to hear,
   At night let it lull me to sleep,
In its murmurs, though drear, there's music to cheer,
   When my heart seems melting to weep.

I long to walk by the surf-beaten shore,
   And to gaze o'er the watery main
Which beats on the strand of my own native land,
   That never shall know me again ;
For tho' a poor exile, wandering afar,
   Unfriended, unloved I must roam,
My heart ever yearns and longingly turns
   To the ocean-bound isle of my home.

Then marvel ye not that I sigh for a place
   On the shores of the deep, blue sea,
For each billow that gleams a messenger seems
   From the land that is dearest to me ;
And I hear in each breeze that comes o'er the seas,
   The voice of a loved one fair,
Who, waiting so long for her lover's return,
   Has gone to her grave in despair.

And now all the joy in life that I ask,
  Is to walk and muse by the sea,
Whose every low surge is a funeral dirge
  For that loved one now lost to me ;
And to gaze o'er the main, with longings tho' vain,
  And to mingle my tears with the wave
Which the tides in their sweep should bear o'er the
    deep,
  To moisten the grass on her grave.

DRIFTING AWAY.

Drifting, drifting, every day,
Down life's current, drifting away ;
Kings and slaves—the grave and the gay,
All on board and drifting away.

Both **saints and sinners** all the same,
The men unknown, and men of fame ;
All the cowards, **and** all the brave,
Are drifting onward to the grave.

Nor love nor wealth their course **can stay,**
Not even a year, nor **yet a day ;**
Whilst some drift fast, **drift others** slow,
But drifting onward all must go.

Youth and beauty cannot avail,
Nor earthly powers can aught prevail ; ·
No priestly prayers, nor precious gift
Can stay the tide on which we drift.

Hear that poor mother how she pleads,
With broken, wounded heart that bleeds ;
For little loved one gone to rest
From its weak moorings at her breast.

And hear the father's anguish wild,
In mourning for that precious child ;
But father's grief nor mother's pain
Can call their loved one back again.

Mark yon pale cheek with hectic flush,
Where passion once was wont to blush ;
And all love's fervency portray,
Now soon in death to drift away.

What tho' her lover's heart should break,
What tho' he'd die for her dear sake ;
His breaking heart no anchor proves,
To stay the tide on which she moves.

The young, the old, the high, the low,
A drifting down this stream must go ;
'Neath spreading sails of deathly pall
This voyage must be made by all.

The **sea to** which we **hither trend**,
With every foe and **every friend**;
Is that dark, shoreless, **boundless sea**,
The **dark,** unknown eternity!

IN PARADISE.

Dedicated **to my friend, Dr. P. K. McMiller.**

In a deep, unbroken forest, beside a flowing stream,
I laid **me down** one afternoon, and, sleeping had a
    dream;
The pearly gates of **paradise** were open to my **view,**
And I saw therein **the faces** that once on earth I
    knew.

No jeweled king **or** beaded priest did there my vision
    trace,
No warrior with his sword and plume, with epaulets
    and lace;
No tattered coat on pauper's back, no miser with his
    gold,
Nor any signs of earthly pomp did I therein behold.

But **every** one was robed alike, **both** of great and
    lowly birth—

Only crowns of different lustre told their stage of virtuous worth,
And those who had ten talents sat nearer to the
throne
Than did the more unfortunate, who never had but
one.

For in Heaven, as on earth, talents supremely reign,
For God loves wisdom better than he does a shallow
brain ;
And according as the talents are improved, which
he has given,
So must be their lot and rank with the angel hosts of
Heaven   .

Some brighter far than others shone, but all were
bright with grace,
No cloud of grief on any brow could there my vision
trace ;
I saw the Christian and the Jew, united hand in
hand,
Dwelling in unbroken peace in that celestial land.

I saw distinctive features of every human race,
And types of every nation in that sweet, holy place ;
Yes, there were men of every tribe, of every rank
and creed,
Whose tasks on earth had been to do their great
Creator's meed.

10

I saw the wild barbarian, and the untaught heathen
 there,
Who were not saved by water, by crucifix nor
 prayer ;
All dwelt in peace together, from priestly hells apart,
For God had known their talents, and judged them
 by the heart.

In supremacy of justice, and in mercy's boundless
 sway,
God, with love and charity, had swept their sins
 away.
And there, in blissful union, where troubles ne'er
 appall,
They praised the great Jehovah, whose hand had
 saved them all.

Yes, he who made this world, 'mid ten thousand
 worlds to roll,
Whose hands created heaven, and man with deathless
 soul,
Who controlls the mighty oceans, which stretch from
 pole to pole,
Never made or framed a creed to damn a human soul.

JACK FROST.

Old Jack Frost has come, his footprints are seen
O'er broad grassy plains that were lately so green,
And, kissed by his lips, his cold, icy breath
Has left on the forests the shadows of death;
And the few gentle flowers yet left us in bloom,
Are drooping like angels knelt over a tomb;
But the ripe, golden fruit, which summer has left,
Requites us for all that its beauties bereft;
And this but illustrates a fact that I've seen,
When loved ones have gone like the summer's bright
    green,
They to Heaven may go, or to ———, just where they
    please,
But the gold which they leave doth all sorrow ap-
    pease.

.

LOVE.

An Acrostic.

Love, oh, thou heart-consuming flame,
Inspired not by wealth or fame,
Zest of every noble claim,
Zealous in thy boundless aim,
Inspiration taught thy name,
Eternal Gods thy wealth proclaim.

Purest type from Heaven's mould,
On maiden's lips thou art extolled,
Wisdom to thy precepts fold,
Evinced through life's endearing hold,
Rejected not by young nor old,
Sure, all thy strength was never told.

FORGET ME NOT.

Forget me not whilst memory's chain
    Holds sacred, firm and true,
Nor let thy heart be steeped in pain
    If I can bear its pain for you.

Forget me not whilst in thy heart
    Thy life's blood ebbs and flows,
Nor let from thee my name depart—
    Forbid me not to share thy woes.

Forget me not where 'erst thou be,
    Whatsoever fate be thine,
On desert's shore or lonely sea,
    Remember love that I am thine.

Forget me not when shades of death
    Shall dwell upon thy breast,
But with thy last departing breath,
    Remember me who loves thee best.

BLITHESOME LITTLE LIBBY.

Pretty little skating girl,
Fairest in the mazy whirl,
Winsome, charming and as fair
And graceful as bird of air—
Blithesome little Libby.

Pretty little skating belle,
Playful as a young gazelle,
Brightly beams, her hazel eyes
As around the rink she flies,
Blithesome little Libby

Pretty little skating queen,
Fairer form was never seen,
Like a vision in a dream—
Memories of her doth seem—
Blithesome little Libby.

LINES TO DORA.

For three long years of toil and strife,
 But one impulse hath filled my breast,
One only aim has been my life,
 An only hope my heart hath blest.

But should I now that impulse name,
 Or breathe the aim my life hath held,
Alas, 'twould be but to proclaim
 That impulse, aim, and hope, dispelled.

For thou on whom I gazed with pride,
 To whom I gave my constant heart,
Hath at the last thy love denied
 And bid me from thy thoughts depart.

With coldness thou hast spurned my love
 And wrung my heart with keenest pain,
But, by the Gods! in time I'll prove
 What thou hast lost by thy disdain.

TILL I COME BACK AGAIN.

No, I'll not forget you darling,
　　Though roaming far away,
Your loving smile shall light my path
　　Wherever I may stray ;
And every loving word of thine
　　Shall e'er with me remain,
And banish every gloomy thought
　　Till I come back again.

The many happy days with you
　　Were all too quickly past,
They were so full of blissful joy
　　I knew they could not last ;
But in my heart a star of hope
　　Shines, not I trust in vain,
And by its light I'll steer my course
　　Till I come back again.

In lands afar beyond the sea
　　My fate may be to roam,
And weeks and months and years may pass
　　Ere I turn back to home ;
But thy bright face in memory set
　　Shall never dim nor wane,
Or lose its charm to light my soul
　　Till I come back again

'Tis only for your sake, my dear,
　　That I must leave you now,

So let me kiss and clear away
    The clouds upon your brow,
Then with your blessing let me go,
    Stern fortune's smiles to gain,
And vow once more, you'll constant prove
    Till I come back again.

Then should misfortunes overtake
    And pall me with dismay,
This thought a talisman shall be
    To break all evil's sway.
It is your promise to be mine,
    And like some sweet refrain
Will ever echo in my heart,
    Till I come back again.

Now, au revoir, but not farewell,
    With one last kiss of love,
To be a seal upon the vow
    That you will constant prove,
And that no other loving swain
    Shall in your heart obtain
The place that I so fondly claim
    Till I come back again.

WELCOME SONG.

All hail! Great Incohonee,
  Great Sachem, wise and true,
Our warriors, braves and chieftains
  Most gladly welcome you,
In Freedom and in Friendship
  United firm and strong,
We gladly hail our chieftain,
  With this our Welcome song.

Chorus—

    Then welcome to our wigwam,
      Our hearts are warm and true,
    Come share our corn and venison,
      And drink our skila-wa-boo.

Within these fertile valleys,
  And on these verdant plains,
The tomahawk we've buried
  And peace and plenty reigns.
Our paths but lead to pleasure,
  No war whoop here resounds,
And now we bid you welcome,
  To these our hunting grounds,

Chorus—

Our hunters are the truest
  That ever grasped a bow,
Our warriors are the bravest

That ever faced a foe.
Our squaws and our papooses,
  And all our maidens bright,
Will hail you, Incohonee,
  With rapture and delight.

Chorus—

MY LOSAHATCHIE* HOME.

In these times of awful panic
  (Strikes are heard of everywhere),
While congress sits and piddles,
  And starvation seems to stare,
When all business goes to pieces
  And the devil 's on a tear,
In vain I long for refuge
  From my troubles and my care.

And my heart is filled with longing
  For that dear old mountain stream,
Losahatchie, on whose surface,
  Like a vision in a dream,
I can always see reflected
  Mount Coloma's rugged dome,
And the little vine-clad cottage
  That I used to call my home.

Even now in heart I'm longing
  To go back there once more,
And with line and pole to wander
  All along its shady shore,
Where, as a careless, barefoot boy,
  I once was wont to roam,
When life was free from sorrow,
  In my Losahatchie home.

O! the promises that wooed me,
  And lured me from that stream,
How false, and, oh! how empty
  Those promises now seem.
All the promised wealth and honors
  That e'en tempted me to roam,
I would gladly now relinquish
  For my Losahatchie home.

Yes, my dear old Losahatchie!
  Since I wandered from thy shore,
The world has not all seemed to be
  What I dreamed in days of yore.
And thy cooling shades and fountains,
  And thy vales of fertile loam
Now fills my soul with longing
  For my Losahatchie home.

Yes, yes; oh, Losahatchie!
  Thou queen of mountain streams,
How often I revisit thee

In my nightly troubled dreams,
To lave my fevered temples
In thy cooling spray and foam,
'Neath thy spreading beech and maples,
At my Losahatchie home.

*Losahatchie is the name of a beautiful mountain stream in North
Alabama.

THE VALE OF LOSAHATCHIE.

O, the vale of Losahatchie,
How I long to be there now,
To bathe my fevered temples
And to cool my aching brow,
In the clear and limpid waters
Of the old Coloma's spring,
And to rest within the shade,
While the birds above me sing.

I am tired with the tumult
Of the city's noisy din ;
With the struggle for existence,
And the babbling tongues of men,
And I long for that old valley,
With its peace and plenty blest,
And to make my home once more
In the old parental nest.

No breaking banks could bring dismay
   In that old valley grand ;
With plow I'd write my honest checks
   And drafts on fertile land,
While that great banker, nature's God,
   Whose wealth is seas and main,
Would principal and interest pay
   Tenfold in golden grain.

And when old Sol had ploughed his course
   Across the heavenly way,
And old Coloma's mountain top
   Lit up with golden ray ;
How sweet would be my night's repose
   And undisturbed my dream,
Soothed there by notes of nightingale,
   And lulled by murmuring stream.

HAIL ST. PATRICK'S DAY.

Dedicated to the members of Emmet Club and my many esteemed
Irish friends.

Hail ! all hail, St. Patrick's day !
  And hail to Erin's glory,
A matchless land, of heroes grand,
  Who live in song and story.
O, patron saint of wondrous land,
  Thy name shall be immortal,
And light the way through endless day
  To Heaven's blessed portal.

Oh, sainted man of wondrous mind,
  Filled with an inspiration,
By Heaven lent and Heaven sent
  To civilize a nation.
And where on earth is there a land
  To-day that does not claim
On history's page some saint or sage—
  Some glorious Irish name ?

And hail ! all hail ! to that green flag,
  Old Erin's sacred treasure ;
Four hundred years, through strife and tears
  And bloodshed without measure,
It floats to-day without a stain,
  An alien though it be,
A tale to tell of freedom's knell,
  As doth the flag of Lee.

Yes, hail! all hail! to Erin's flag,
  Exiled though now it be,
In other climes and other times
  That flag shall yet be free,
And float as proudly to the breeze
  As when unfurled of yore,
For God's decreed it shall be freed
  And float forevermore!

Then hark! oh, hark, ye Irish sons!
  Behold your country bleeding,
While saints above and sires you love
  With you her cause is pleading,
And bid you, by the sacred ties
  Of all that's dear on earth,
To break in twain the tyrant's chain,
  And free your land of birth.

Then grasp, oh, grasp the glorious flag
  That bears no blot of shame,
And swear by love of God above
  And by St. Patrick's name,
That you will ne'er forsake its cause
  'Till it in triumph waves,
That o'er the foam you'll bear it home,
  Or bear it to your graves.

THE EVENING PRAYER.

'Twas grandma taught our little girl,
Our four·year darling May,
Her "Now I lay me down to sleep,"
On bended knee to pray.
"If I should die before I wake,
I pray the Lord my soul to take;"
And then to close the evening prayer,
Would have her add thereto:
God bless my grandma Smith,
Grandpa Smith and Uncle Joe,
My grandpa White and grandma White,
And (other names) good night.

One evening at her grandma's knee,
When tired out with play,
The little darling bowed her head
Her evening prayer to say,
She finished out the little rhymes,
And blessings then began,
With "damma Smith and dampa White,
And dampa Smith," and here the light
Shut out by drooping lids,
She added in her innocence,
(Without thought of fun or jokes),
"Dam—dam—and all my dam tinfolkes."

11

"OUR ORDER HERE."

In response to a toast.

But I forget.   'Tis not of our fair city and her
matchless wealth, by lavish hand of God bestowed,
that I would speak,

But 'tis of something nobler, far—
A jewel bright—a shining star—
The brightest gem which decks her brow,
Is that which I would champion now.
But should I speak, as well I might,
Of furnaces whose fires bright
Make noonday of our darkest night
And paint the skies with lurid light,
Or tell how wondrous here combine
The wealth of coal and iron mines,
And how our manufactures great
The riches bring from every State ;
Or, boastful, tell in wondrous tale
The matchless glories of this vale,
Your pardon just I might receive,
Tho' some, perchance, would scarce believe,
For such the story 'twould but seem
Like fiction or a summer's dream.
But, as I said, 'tis not of these
I'll speak ; my hearers now to please.
A grander theme my soul inspires
And warms me with ennobling fires,
My theme is of our order grand.

The noblest in this glorious land.
And tho' our numbers are but few,
Each Knight is valiant, brave and true,
And counts but wasted ev'ry sun
Which sees not some good action done,
Some noble act or generous deed
In keeping with our order's creed,
For Knights of Honor ever hold
Kind actions more than finest gold.
To shield the widows and provide
For orphans is our greatest pride;
To raise the fallen, help the weak,
And dry the tear on mourner's cheek;
To help our brothers in distress,
And ev'ry home we enter, bless;
To carry sunshine and relief
Wherever hang the clouds of grief,
Reviving hope and stilling fear,
These are our daily missions here.
To sit beside the bed of pain
When fever burns a brother's brain
And nurse him back to health again.
From works like these we ne'er refrain,
And when our great dictator, God,
Bids brother Knight pass 'neath the rod
And enter that grand lodge on high—
That lodge supreme, above the sky—
We fold his hands upon his breast,
And when his corpse with prayer we've blest,
We give him cortege to the grave

And there with tears his dust we lave.
And flowers strew upon his bier.
I speak this, of our Order here.

A FRAGMENT.

Let angels that hover around us in air
   Keeping record of joys that bloom in the heart,
Proclaim from their tablets the dearest joy there,
   And in whispers of spirit we'll hear them impart;
That it is the sweet pleasure when exiles we roam
   Of knowing that loved ones remember us still—
And that dear ones we've left behind us at home
   Have thoughts of ourselves their memories to fill.

HUMOR

AND

DIALECT.

I THINK I THUNK A LIE.

I used to think when I was young,
  And my heart was free from guile,
That there was grief in every tear
  And joy in every smile ;
That friendship was not all a cheat
  And love could never die,
But thinking now of what I thunk,
  I think I thunk a lie.

I used to think about myself,
  And think that I would be
A governor or a president,
  Or a general like Lee ;
But I have waited long in vain,
  Whilst years rolled slowly by,
And, thinking now of what I thunk,
  I think I thunk a lie.

I used to think the ladies were
  All sweetnesses combined,
That they were all God's last and best
  Of perfectness refined ;
That they were not half pads and paint,
  But angels from on high,
But, thinking now of what I thunk,
  I think I thunk a lie.

The preachers, too, I used to think,
  Were not like other men,

And were not tempted of the flesh,
  And could not, therefore, sin ;
But since I've traveled round a bit
  I've watched them on the sly,
And, thinking now of what I thunk,
  I think I thunk a lie.

The honest tiller of the soil,
  When marketing his crop,
Takes pains to put the ripe and best
  Always upon the top ;
I used to think those honest men
  Would never cheat nor try,
But, thinking now of what I thunk.
  I think I thunk a lie.

The editors, a lordly set,
  Who live on milk and honey,
They've nothing else on earth to do
  But write and rake in money ;
Leastwise, that way I used to think,
  But now it makes me cry,
To think about the way I thunk,
  And how I thunk a lie.

What noble men the doctors are,
  I used to think they came
From Heaven or some heavenly land
  And worked for love or fame ;
That they could cure all human ills,
  And never let us die,

But, thinking now of what I thunk,
  I think I thunk a lie.

The lawyers, too, I used to think,
  Oh, God, forgive the thought,
That their convictions of the right
  Could not by knaves be bought;
That they would not a client rob,
  Or "sell" him on the sly,
But, thinking now of what I thunk,
  I think I thunk a lie.

The dry-goods men were honest, too,
  They'd swear they sold at cost,
I used to think they told the truth,
  And all their profits lost;
I thought a yard was full three feet,
  Don't ask my reasons why,
But, thinking now of what I thunk,
  I think I thunk a lie.

The hotel clerk, I used to think,
  Would try to be polite,
Would answer questions put to him,
  And treat a stranger right;
And rather than he'd play the ass
  That he would sooner die,
But, thinking now of what I thunk,
  I think I thunk a lie.

The democrats, I used to think,
  It once they got the floor
Would turn the dirty rascals out,
  And kick 'em from the door;
That they would stop the tariff steal
  That piles the surplus high,
But, thinking now of what I thunk,
  I think I thunk a lie.

And then I thought that Harrison,
  Who took old Grover's shoes,
Would have the backbone and the grit
  To give us all our dues;
But tariff laws and pension frauds
  Still make the nation sigh,
And, thinking now of what I thunk,
  I think I thunk a lie.

I used to think elections were
  The public will to voice,
And not a thimble-rigging game
  To give the cliques their choice;
That patriotism played its part,
  Tho' stills were never dry,
But, thinking now of what I thunk,
  I think I thunk a lie.

I used to think that public schools,
  Would fill a long-felt need,
By teaching all our boys and girls
  How to write, spell and read;

But red tape and their rottenness
　　Is everywhere the cry,
And, when I think of what I thunk,
　　I think I thunk a lie.

The niggers, too, I used to think,
　　If once they were set free,
Would make good, honest citizens,
　　Like white folks used to be ;
But they have wandered far from grace,
　　The chickens still roost high,
And, thinking now of what I thunk,
　　I think I thunk a lie.

I used to think the town police,
　　With all its blue and brass,
Would never sleep upon his post,
　　Nor let a criminal pass ;
That on " blind tigers " they would keep
　　An ever watchful eye,
But, thinking now of what I thunk,
　　I think I thunk a lie.

Our prison house, I used to think,
　　A model kind of jail,
That they who'd try its walls to break
　　Would most assuredly fail,
That guardsmen there to duty sworn
　　Would ne'er let prisoner fly,
But, thinking now of what I thunk,
　　I think I thunk a lie.

I used to think the poor Chinee
　　Was worse than "Melican man,"
That we should missionaries send
　　With civilization's plan;
But thinking now of late events
　　Beneath our Southern sky,
I rather think that what I thunk
　　Was "wusser" than a lie.

SERMON BY UNCLE MOSE.
No. 1.

My belubbed cullud brudders,
　　Havin' lef at home my specks,
I'll hav ter ax yer pardin
　　Fer not readin' ob my tex;
But yer'll fine de inspirasion
　　Ob what I has ter say
In de pistle ob de postle
　　To de church in Africa.

De language arr explicit,
　　An' dis is what it am:
Er man shud git er hustle on
　　An' be not like er clam.
So please ter give attention,
　　An' try ter keep erwake

Whilse I de applicasion
　　Will now attempt ter make.

Now de fust ting I must tell yer,
　　An' I gits it from my tex,
Er clam's no good for dis yer worl',
　　Nor fitten for de nex;
He's er lazy, stupid creetur—
　　Yes, dats jess what he am—
An' er man shud git er hustle on,
　　An' be not like er clam.

Now ter hustle am ter rustle,
　　An' ter rustle means ter work;
So w'en yer's got er job ter do
　　Yer shudn't orter shirk,
But lay rite hole wid hones' lick
　　As hard as yer can lam,
Fer a man shud git er hustle on,
　　An' be not like er clam.

All yer jinin' ob societies,
　　An' marchin' roun' wid flags,
Ain't at all er gwinter help yer
　　Keep yer familys outer rags,
Fer behine yer grips an' signuls,
　　Yer flip-flops an' flim-flams,
Dere's some hustler after nickels
　　In de pockets ob de clams.

An' dis talk erbout dem pawn shops,
　　De new sub-treasury scheme,

Is er snare an' er delusion
   An' er empty-headed dream,
An' yer'll fine when yer hab waited,
   Dats its but er trickster's sham ;
So yer wants ter git er hustle on,
   An' be not like a clam.

When de wily politician
   Comes er roun' ter get yer vote,
An' vites yer ter de barbicue,
   To eat de roasted shote;
When he puts his arms er roun' yer
   An' begs yer take er dram,
Yer had better git er hustle on,
   An' be not like er clam.

Fer as sho as I'se er preachin'
   When de 'lection day is pass,
An' dat politician's 'lected,
   An' yer craps are in de grass,
He will scorn yer an' will spurn yer,
   Fer de fool he kno's yer am,
An' yer'll wish yer'd kept er hustlin'
   An' been not like er clam.

Er word now in conclusion,
   While we pass er roun' de hat,
Yer wants ter git er hustle on
   When we shall cum ter dat.
Let some one grine de organ
   An' start us up er psalm—
Please, brudders, git er hustle on,
   An' be not like er clam.

SERMON BY UNCLE MOSE.
No. 2.

My belubbed cullud brudders,
  Ise gwine ter preach ter day,
An' I hopes ter hab attention
  Ter what Ise gwine ter say.
I know dere's room for provement
  In ebery sinner's hart,
An' my reason fur so thinkin'
  I will now ter you impart.

First, de selfishness of nater
  Keeps de hart from gitten clean ;
It blinds de eyes of conscience
  An' makes us over-mean ;
It puts er man ter thinkin'
  Dat he's better dan de best,
An' like a tyrant robber,
  Drives the goodness from his breast.

An' den dere is er kind er pride
  Dat steals into de brain
An' robs er man of reason
  An' makes him weak an' vain ;
An' when er man has got it,
  He is saddled mity well,
Fur de debil den ter mount him
  An' ter ride him inter hell.

Den dere's anudder passion
　An' de Scripter calls it lust,
An' if any o' you's got it
　You is hardly fit ter trust.
'Tis de pizen ob er sarpint,
　So polutin ter de soul,
Dat de meanness ob its venom
　De debil would extole.

An' den de sin ob appetite,
　Since ob dat I cum ter think,
It's de bebil's own invension
　When it leads er man ter drink ;
It destroys all his conscience,
　Puts er blind upon his eyes
An' empties him ob character,
　An' fills him up wid lies.

A word now in conclusion
　Ob what Ise had ter say,
A preacher cannot lib on wind,
　He orter hab his pay.
So while you hunt yer nickles
　An' we pass eround de hat,
Please see dey isn't counterfits,
　Be sho you look ter dat.

SPEECH OF UNCLE MOSE.

My fren's and culled citizens,
　　I'm er gwine ter make er speech,
And I wants ter hab de 'tention
　　Ob all in hearin' reach.
My words are nuts o' wizdum,
　　Shucked clean ob all de hulls,
And I hope dey'll find a lodgement
　　In de hollers ob yer skulls.

Dis am de white man's country,
　　And dat nigger am er fool
Who thinks de white folks gwinter
　　Low de culled folks ter rule ;
For de Massachusetts Yankee
　　An' de Southern democrat
Am united same as brudders
　　On de politix ob dat.

You may shout yerselves plum outer breff,
　　And cut yer bigest figers,
A whoopin' fer dem candidates
　　Who say dey love de niggers ;
But you write it down wid charcoal
　　And jes keep it fer er rule,
You'll never gain by politix
　　Forty acres and er mule.

When Marse Lincun gave us freedom,
　　'Twant no freedom fur ter steal,

But to earn an hones' libbin
  By a grubbin' in de fiel',
And when dat proclamation
  Ole hones' Abram wrote
He neber thought a nigger
  Would git rich upon his vote.

And now I wants ter 'vise yer,
  While a talkin' on dat line,
You better quit yo politix
  And de granger's party jine;
Den you can eat yer chickens,
  'Thout ketchin' 'em at night,
And when yer see a p'liceman
  Won't be tremblin' at de sight.

A word now in conclusion,
  To you upper crusty coons,
Wid yo fancy walkin' canes
  And yer striped pantaloons;
You better git yerselves ter work,
  And stop yo braggin' sass,
'Fore some white man's cungeration
  Lays you out below de grass.

SHAMS AND SHACKS.

Mankind is not just what it seems,
  This world is half made up of shams,
Some men as silent sages pose
  Who are at best but stupid clams.

Some babbling tongues are never still,
  Misquoting thoughts of wiser men,
And in their self-esteem suppose
  That they are what they've never been.

Some noble hearts as ever beat
  Pulsate in breasts of rugged mould,
Whilst broadcloth often wraps the knave
  Whose sins and crimes are never told.

Some glorious poets live and die,
  And ne'er to wealth or fame are known,
Whilst fools are flattered to the sky
  For genius that was not their own.

Yes, more than half mankind are fools,
  Hence knaves and fools find easy sailing,
To hug a sham and be humbugged
  Is with the mass a common failing.

I've known a rum-besotted quack,
  High in the healing arts to pass,
Whose intellect was scarce above
  The instincts of a stupid ass.

And oft a tailless ape we see
　　Whose only brain is brazen cheek,
High-seated on judicial bench
　　To judge the fools who justice seek.

And sometimes, too, in sacred desk
　　A wolf we find in sheep's attire,
Too cowardly to preach the truth,
　　But preaching hell without a fire.

And so it goes throughout the world,
　　Hypocrisy is ruling still,
A man is boosted going up,
　　And kicked when coming down the hill.

Angelic woman, sweet and pure,
　　When wedded to a worthless clown,
By gravity of social laws,
　　Are to his level anchored down.

But sometimes wilful, wicked wives,
　　Make noblest husbands hump and hustle,
And he's a fool who thinks to find
　　An angel wrapped with every bustle.

HURRAH FOR THE ROAD!

"Good news for Rome," the head-lines sed
  And then four columns follered,
Which, after which when I had read,
  I jist stood up and hollered.

Three cheers, sed I, for that great man
  Who allers holds his tung,
And never blows erbout er plan
  Till success ter it is brung.

One man like him, I'll tell yer what,
  Is wuth his weight in gole;
The kind of good, hoss sense he's got
  Is the simmon reaching pole.

He bleves in action more than blab,
  And he's got that kind of grit
That makes the croker hush his gab,
  And hustlers git up and git.

Then here's to Williamson, three cheers!
  Let his praise the welkin ring;
A friend to Rome he has no peers,
  Long live the Railroad King!

PEPPER SAUCE.

Times now ain't like they used to be,
  There's change in every thing;
Even the dollars of our daddies
  Have lost their old-time ring.

Our sugar now is mixed with sand,
  Of paper shoes are made;
There's fraud in measures and in weights,
  In every line of trade.

The farmer used to own his land
  And lived on all the best,
But now the merchant owns the farm
  With its smoke-house in the West.

No mortgage clause was on the notes
  Which our daddies used to pay,
But now they bind up everything,
  From crops to dinner tray.

We used to have good, honest laws—
  Laws made for honest men,
But now our code's so full of flaws
  It's hardly worth a pin.

Few honest statesman can we find,
  The demagogue now rules,
And everywhere in halls of state
  We meet with knaves and fools.

With homestead laws they've gulled the poor,
   And exemption statutes framed,
'Till thievery they've legalized,
   And justice made ashamed.

The honest poor man's credit's gone,
   His word ain't worth a mote,
And now to get his wife a shroud
   He must sign a mortgage note.

THE GUITAR.

I 'member way back long ago,
  Fore de Yankees sot us free,
A nigger wid an old banjo
  Was happy as can be;
But looking back to dem ole times,
  Way back befo' de war.
I wonder how dem niggers did
  Widout a light guitar.

Wid rattle bones and ole banjo
  Dey used to play and sing,
And dance befo' de cabin do,
  An cut de pigeon wing;
But dem ole days am pass and gone,
  De banjo ain't nowhar;
De niggers now mus' put on airs
  And pick de light guitar,

Dese am de halleluja times,
  Our work am turned to play;
We ain't got nuffin else to do
  But frolic night and day;
Our corn-field hands are turned to dudes,
  De wash-women "ladies" are,
De banjo it am laid aside,
  While we pick de light guitar.

Each nigger in de barber shop.
  And ebery hotel coon

Is trumming on de light guitar,
    An' trying to play er tune ;
But by and by dem kinkey heads
    Will be hustled on de kyars
And bundled off to Mexico,
    Along wid dere guitars.

For white folks now am gitten tired
    Ob sich hyfalutin' style,
An' when dere patience gits threadbare
    Dere blood am gwine ter bile ;
An if dem kinkey-headed coons
    Keeps on wid sich fool airs,
Dey'l lan' in h—l or Mexico,
    Erlong wid dere guitars.

THE DUDE.

There's a fellow in this city,
   I guess you know him well,
But if not 'tis no pity,
   For he's but a fancy swell,
Who only lives for pleasure,
   A life of ease and rest.
And of all his mammy's children,
   He loves himself the best.

You'll find him at the races,
   The party and soiree,
And in the ladies' faces
   He fondly looks to see
A smiling recognition
   Of his form so finely drest,
For of all his mammy's children,
   He loves himself the best.

He drives the finest horses
   And dances with much grace.
Tho' in his weazen features
   The monkey you can trace.
He's a four-ply base ball critic,
   At billiards plays with zest,
And of all his mammy's children,
   He loves himself the best.

But at the ball and picnic
   This la da da young dude

Gets in his finest antics,
  His monkey actions rude ;
A crank he is on waltzing
  With a dudine on his breast,
For of all his mammy's children,
  He loves himself the best.

I guess the God who made him
  Must have made him for a cause,
But really I'm too shallow
  To imagine what it was ;
His head I know is empty,
  No virtue fills his breast,
But of all his mammy's children,
  He loves himself the best.

COURAGE AND AMBITION.

Ef I wus but er tadpole—
  Er tadpole weak and frail—
I wud strive ter be a frog,
  Do I neber shed my tail.

An' befo' I'd be er clam,
  Allers shet up outer sight,
I wud bust my shell ersunder,
  Do I perished in de light.

Yes, I rudder be er flyin' squerel,
  Ter fly er while an' fall,
Dan be er lazy tarepin
  An' do nothin' else but crawl.

An' ef I wusn't bigger
  Dan er little yaller ant
I wud exercise er courage
  Equel tu de elephant ;

Fer I hold dat it is noble,
  An' ercordin' ter God's plan,
Dat man in ebery station
  Shud prove hissef er man.

Dat de only true nobility
  Is by hones' labor wrought,
An' er crown dat's wuf de wearin'
  Is by mortal neber bought.

An' I can't help hate er croaker,
  Wid his weak an' watery eyes
Allers turned towards de groun',
  Neber raised toward de skies;

Who goes erbout complainin'
  An' bemoanin' ob his fate,
Because he is er ninny
  Instid ob sumpin' great;

Who neber makes an effort
  Ter reach er noble hight,
But hides his ebery talent
  In his bosom outer sight,

An' bows in weak submission.
  Like er cringin' yaller houn',
An' licks de hand uplifted
  Ter strike him ter de groun'.

But I glory in de courage
  My convictions ter assert,
An' I'll strive ter be er man
  Do I'se but made ob dirt.

Fer I no de soul widin me
  Is er libin' part ob God,
An' will lib in spheres eternal
  When my form has turned ter sod.

An' as I lub ter honor
  Dat God, who in His plan,
Made me in His image,
  I will strive ter be er man.

DON'T IT SORTER LOOK THAT WAY?

When you see a fancy feller
   Loafing 'round upon the streets,
Allers smoking cigarettes,
   And hobnobin' with dead beats;
While his mother does his washing,
   For which he doesn't pay;
You would take him for a dude—
   Don't it sorter look that way?

An' when he gets ter fishin'
   Or keeps a pinter dog,
He can tell er lie as easy
   As fallen off a log;
Or if he doesn't fabricate
   His imagination's play
Er 'mounts ter 'bout the same—
   Don't it sorter look that way?

And when you go to meetin',
   An' set down in er pew,
An' er gal with monster hat
   Shuts the preacher out from view,
Don't you feel more like cussin'
   Than you do to kneel and pray;
Now railly, if you don't,
   Don't you sorter feel that way?

An' when 'lection time's approachin',
   An' er feller comes er round

Er bowin' an' er scrapin',
    An' er talkin' so profoun'—
Uv the "conflics of opinion,"
    An' "the crisis uv the day,"
He's er hankerin' fur office—
    Don't it sorter look that way?

An' I needn't ter remind you
    That the time has got here when
The finances uv er man
    Hides er mighty heap o' sin;
For if he's got the ducats
    He can kill and he can slay,
An' the jury will excuse him—
    Don't it sorter look that way?

But should you hear a lawyer
    Runnin' other lawyers down,
An' er wearin' of er swagger,
    As if he run the town;
You may bet your bottom dollar,
    He's a jackleg every way,
Or er petifogin' shyster—
    Don't it sorter look that way?

An' when you hear a feller,
    As yer can most any time,
Abusin' some po' doctor,
    An' accusin' him of crime,
You may swar he owes fur physic
    An' don't intend ter pay,

For it allers seems ter happen
  That it's sorter that er way.

And the man that reads er paper
  Fur er year er even more,
An' writes ter stop its comin'
  'Thout settlin' up his score,
He's er dead beat an' er scoundrel
  Who means ter beat his way,
An' the devil's gwine ter get him,
  Don't it sorter look that way?

THE GIRLS OF SILVER CREEK.

"Poeta nascitur non fit,"
Some ancient sage or bard has writ,
But I was not a poet born,
Or if I was, I've spoilt the horn;
At least I'm no poetic spoon,
Or if I am, was pulled too soon;
Nor have I climbed Parnassus' Mount,
Or drunk from Helicon's sweet fount;
Nor do I woo the sacred nine
To aid me in this task of mine,
Nor need I the Pegasus' jade,
For theme like mine should claim no aid.
I need no Latin, French or Greek

To praise the girls of Silver Creek.
Their charms alone my pen inspire
And lifts me from prosaic mire,
That I must tread when praising men,
Or telling facts "that might have been,"
I'll drink not e'en the ruby wine
To wake within me thoughts divine;
But trusting naught for inspiration,
I'll write as suits my inclination.
Let critics mouthe and criticise,
'Tis critics that I most despise.
Fools find it easier faults to find
Than their own business ends to mind;
But hang it all! this long prelude
Is wasting time and does no good.
So, girls, here goes, know I'm your friend,
I hope to please and not offend.
The first of whom I'll sing is Matt,
She's full of fun and awful fat;
Where'er she goes it's "get out sadness,"
Make room for fun, good will and gladness.
She's a sugar lump of sweetest joys,
And weighs two hundred avoirdupois.
The next is Georgia, her fair sister,
A kiss from whom would raise a blister;
She's neat and tidy as a pin,
And has a heart that knows no sin.
That she's a beauty, bet your life,
And would make a man a noble wife.
And there is Annie—she's a daisy,

Enough to run a lover crazy.
She's young and gentle, sweet and tender,
A lovely blonde, graceful, slender;
Her lips with ripe twin cherries vie,
And roses bow when she goes by.
Then Jennie R., the little fairy,
Bashful, timid, and so wary;
To flatter her was just as silly
As trying to paint the fairest lily.
But what shall I of Julia say?
Would I a worthy tribute pay
To her kind heart and gen'rous soul,
I'd need the Heavens for a scroll.
On less of space I could not find
Room to praise her heart so kind;
But so much space can't be her meed,
The will is given for the deed.
And now the next is Etta's name,
To wake my soul's poetic flame;
And as I clasp my willing pen,
To praise this fairy of the glen,
My thoughts run wild, my heart beats high,
But to flatter her I need not try;
Her charms no pen can panegyrize,
But he who wins her wins a prize.
And then there's Ida, whom we miss,
To have her back would give us bliss.
There 're many hearts will sigh and ache
'Till she returns, for her sweet sake.

13

Nor Lizzie B. will I omit,
When praising beauty, worth and wit;
For those are graces all her own,
And thousands more I can't make known.
Nor would I here Miss Lula slight,
For slighting her would not be right.
She's full of goodness, pluck and grit,
And knows the rule, "git up and git."
I cannot praise her worth too much,
The world were better for more just such—
But like the dessert after dinner,
As sure as I'm an honest sinner,
I've left the best to be the last,
In winding up my rhyme's repast.
'Tis Emma W., she's a whizzer,
A thousand boys would like to squeeze her,
For she's so plump, so sweet and fair,
Tom I——n sighs to be a bear.
But Tom, old boy, you need not sigh,
The best of grapes are always high;
The sweetest sugar's in hard lumps,
And queens are caught by bigger trumps;
So sail in Tom, with all the rest,
For he who wins is more than blest.

A SPRING CANT-OH.

I do not claim to be a saint,
   Filled with amazing grace,
Nor boast of sanctifying love
   For all the human race :
But like most other mortals be
   That's born for wearing pants,
I am full to overflowing
   With a great many can'ts.

I can't help feeling when I sit
   In the temple of the Lord
And listen to a preacher's tongue,
   Whose every studied word
Is meant to gain a compliment
   From some dudine in her pew,
That he's a sorter hypocrit ;
   I can't, oh, can you?

And when I pay my dollar cash
   For a seat in the parquet,
And go with great anxiety
   To hear and see the play,
And have to sit behind a hat
   That hides the stage from view,
I can't help feeling cross as sin ;
   I can't, oh, can you?

And when I hear a fellow pray,
   "Lord let thy kingdom come,"

And see him straightway cast his vote
  For the licensed sale of rum,
I guess he means just what he prays
  And votes to prove it true,
But somehow I can't see the point;
  I can't, oh, can you?

And when I'm told the human race
  Is all from Adam's seed,
That kinkey-headed coons and I
  Are from one common breed,
I think that apes and darn baboons
  Must be my brothers too;
But then I can't believe the tale;
  I can't, oh, can you?

'Tis said that wicked Birmingham
  Is not a friend to grace;
That every dweller in its bounds
  Is heading for that place
Where water works are never known
  And ice supplies are scant;
But I don't think it's wholly true,
  I can't, oh, I can't.

I'm also told that demagogues
  Have caught the hayseed vote;
Are piloting and steering, too,
  The new Alliance boat;
That they are going to take the earth
  And everything in view,
But I don't hardly think they will;
  I can't, oh, can you?

UNCLE MOSE ON THE PRODIGAL'S RETURN.

I don't go much on brag an' blow,
　An' all dat kind er stuff,
But w'en it comes ter w'at I no
　I gess I noes enuff,
I'se read de Bible tru an' tru,
　An' Watson's commontater,
An' w'at I hasen't got from books
　I'se learned frum common nater.

I'se read er heap er books on law—
　On fisic quite er number,
But de Bible am de book ob books—
　I'll tell yer it's er hummer.
It tells erbout ole Prodigal
　An' his two grown-up boys,
Who uster run er cattle ranch
　Way up in Illinoise.

Now dat ole granger, Prodigal,
　Had ways a little quar,
But w'en it cum ter business,
　He was allers far an' squar.
He neber took ter politics,
　Nor seemed to keer er cent
Who was 'lected Governor,
　Nor who was President.

He tended strictly tu his ranch,
　　An' raised er sight er stock;
He was er hard-shell in belief—
　　His hed was like er rock.
His younges' son wan't bilt dat way,
　　He was lazy like an' rude;
He wudn't plow nor mind de stock,
　　But wanted to be er dude.

So one day w'en he met his dad,
　　Way down beside de branch.
He said: "Ole dad, I wanter cash
　　My interest in de ranch.
In mind I'se made up w'at I'll do,
　　I'll tell yer now my plan—
I'm gwine erway ter some big town
　　An' make myself er man."

De old man stood er while, den said:
　　"I think I see yer game;
Like dat ole sockless Kansas chap,
　　Yer wants ter win er name.
Well, yer shall hab in solid cash
　　Yer hones', riteful share
Ob all de lan', de cows an' sheep,
　　An' ebry thing dats here."

An' so de ole man went ter town
　　An' drawed out from de bank
Enough of gold and silver coin
　　Ter fill er water tank,

An' fotch it home in leather bags,
  An' giv it ter dat boy,
Who almost cut de pigeon wing,
  He was so full ob joy.

Well, dat smart Alec wid his cash
  Lit out upon de kyars
Ter try his luck in Chicago,
  Ermong de buils and bars.
He bought er place in de exchange,
  An' went it strong on wheat,
And what he lost he tried ergin
  Ter make it up on meat.

On cotton nex' he posted up
  Ter give dat game er whack,
Hopin' dat he'd make er deal
  An' win his losses back.
But fortune didn't seem ter smile
  Upon him wuth er cent,
An' every dollar dat he had
  Ter kiver margins went.

His watch an' chain he nex' put up
  Ter raise er final stake,
But lost it on three card monte,
  Played by er circus fake.
Now busted flat as he cud be,
  Widout er single nick,
He had ter ax his boadin' miss
  Ter let him run on tick

But w'en a man is outer cash,
  He's sho' ter loose his smile,
An' soon his boardin' miss foun' out
  Dat he had drapt his pile ;
An' den she bounced him out ob doors,
  Ter loaf upon de street,
An' nex' de free lunch counter man
  Jist bounced him fer er beat.

Ter steer ergin' de vagrant law,
  An' not git floated in,
Was mo' den he cud hope ter do,
  Widout er home or fren' ;
An' so he hid hissef all day,
  Till it was gettin dusk,
Den slipt out ter de slaughter pen
  An' filled hissef on husk.

But second table after hogs
  Was not sich sumpshus fare
As dat young chap cud git at home,
  If he was only dere,
An' so he, talkin' to hissef,
  Said, "I will jist be durn,
Even do I have ter hop cross-ties,
  I'll tu my dad return."

An' so he straightway hit de grit—
  Jist lit out fer his home—
An' 'twasn't many days before
  In sight he'd fairly come.

De ole man, lookin' down de road,
 His wanderin' son espied,
Den run an' fell upon his neck,
 An' sobbed an' blubbering, cried.

Den takin' him inter de house
 Give him his Sunday cote,
His bran new boots an' dimon' ring,
 An' dressed him like er spote.
Fine invitations by him sent
 All roun' de country flew,
Invitin' all his frens ter cum
 Out ter er barbicue.

He sent out fer his oberseer,
 An' bid him quickly kill
De fattes' ox upon de ranch,
 His sons an' frens ter fill.
He sed he didn't keer er cent
 For w'at de worl' might say,
He felt so glad ter see his son
 He'd celebrate de day.

His udder boy w'at stayed at home—
 Young Elder was his name—
Heerd of de racket goin' on
 An' lowed dat he'd be blame
If he was gwinter stan' sich biz—
 It wasn't far nor squar;
Dat he was jist as good as him,
 If he hadn't been no whar.

But w'en de niggers tole old Prod
   W'at Elder had ter say
He lef' de crowd up at de house
   An' hurried right erway
Down to de barn whar Elder was,
   An' ter dat youngster sed:
'' Yer brudder is erlive at home,
   Aldo we thought him ded.''

An' den he went on wid er yarn
   'Bout havin' pleasure most
Ober one old ram dats foun'
   Dan ninety-nine not lost,
An' tried ter taffy up his son
   Wid chestnut tales like dis,
Dat while he stayed at home an' worked
   Dat ebry ting was his.

But Elder was as mad as sheol,
   An' told his daddy plain
He wasn't satisfied er bit;
   Dat he troo sun an' rain
Had stayed at home and done de work
   De whole long summer troo
An' neber eben got er goat,
   Much less er barbicue.

De moral now ter dis yer tale
   Ter me is berry plain;
Ole Prod ought not ter bin so glad
   Ter see dat boy ergain,

Fer as he neber was no good,
But allers breedin' harm,
He ought not ter hab been er lowed
Ter come back on dat farm.

SPEECH OF UNCLE MOSE ON INDEPEND-
ENCE DAY.

My frens and cullud citizens,
Wese ersembled here dis morn
To celebrate de 'casion
W'en liberty wus born ;
W'en de young ermerican eagle
Fust busted fum his shell,
An' give er whoop fer liberty—
Er reg'lar rebel yell.

Dat wus de grandess 'casion
Dat eber bless'd de yearth,
An' nations wus astounded
At de glory ob its birth,
Fer neber in de history
Ob all de ages past
Wus eber such er nation
Fum de molds ob wisdom cast.

An' I tell yer, feller-citizens,
   It makes my busom swell
Wid proudness w'en I read erbout
   Or hear dem speakers tell
Ob how dat unfledg'd eagle
   Girded on de belt ob right
An' challeng'd Englan's lion
   Ter cum out an' hab er fight.

So strong had grown dat bludy beast,
   So puft'd up an' so gran',
He thought hissef de champion
   Ob all de seas an' lan'.
Wid scorn he heard an' look'd upon
   Dat yankee bird so small,
An' swore dat he wud chaw him up—
   Meat, fedders, bones, an' all.

But dat new hatch'd-out yankee bird,
   So seeming small and weak,
Wus hatch'd wid claws as sharp as steel
   An' wid er hole-fas' beak;
His eyes wus full of lightnin' fire,
   His gizzard full ob grit,
An' like young David wid de sling,
   He noed jess whar ter hit.

An', too, our Uncle Sam was dere
   Ter back dat eagle game,
Fer well he knew he cum fum stock
   Dat tyrants cud not tame;

An' quickly kiverin' ebry bet
　　Dat ole John Bull put down,
He cried w'en dat ole bluff refused
　　Ter bet his throne an' crown.

But not because he had er use
　　Fer eny such ole plunder,
He only wished to win de stuff
　　Den kick it in ter thunder,
Dat ebry Englishman might see
　　He did not care er snap
Fer dere ole royal, high-back chair,
　　Nor ole carbuncl'd cap.

At las', in ole Virginia,
　　Dey begun de scrappin' match
While Injuns stood eround an' yell'd
　　Ter see 'em bite and scratch.
Roun' after roun' dey fit an' claw'd,
　　Returnin' lick fer lick,
An' Englan's lion soon found out
　　Dat bird wus hard ter pick.

Dey fit all round ole Lexington,
　　An' roun' Dorchester's hight,
An' plum er cross ole Bunker's hill,
　　Still strugglin' in dere might ;
Till mad wid pain dat lion's roar
　　Wus echo'd far an' wide,
Fer ebry time he cum in reach
　　Dat eagle tore his hide.

He pull'd his mane, he twis' his tail,
   He fill'd his eyes wid san'
Till dat ole lion got so weak
   Dat he cud barly stan';
But still de eagle kep' his lick
   Nor seemed de least dismayed,
For he was boun' dat beast ter lick
   An' lay him in de shade.

But by an' by de sponge went up,
   Dat lion tuck'd his tail,
An' cross'd de broad Atlantic sea
   His losses ter bewail.
De eagle bold den spread his wing
   An' soar'd erway on high
Ter roost ermid de circlin' stars
   An' guard us wid his eye.

An' since de early dawn ob time,
   W'en de sky its robes unfurl'd,
An' de great quire ob Heabenly stars
   Sung er welcom' ter de world;
Since de day-god in his splendor
   Fust look'd down fum on high,
Dere has neber been er 'casion
   Like dat Fourth day ob July.

Er word now in conclusion,
   Ter yer good white folks out dere—
Ef eny ob yer has er dime
   Dat yer kin kindly spare,

Er ef yer chance ter hab at home
   Sum good ole cast off close,
Plese 'member yer ole culled fren,
   Yer hones' Uncle Mose.

A PLEA TO MAYOR LANE.

Please, Mister Lane, do hear my plea
   And grant alleviation,
I'm almost dead, my nerves unstrung,
   My soul's in desperation ;
I've got the spancue and jimjams,
   My brain is worn to pieces
By that infernal hurdy-gurdy
   Whose grinding never ceases.

From early morn till late at night
   That cruel fiend's persistence
In grinding doleful measures out,
   Makes life unworth existence.
I cannot think, I cannot work,
   I scarce can get my breath ;
Do dynamite the blasted thing
   Before it proves my death.

Yes, Mister Mayor, heed my woe
   And banish, by your orders,
That curse-provoking, damned machine,
   Beyond earth's outer borders,
Don't let it drive me on to drink
   To drown my wild despair,
But choke it off and smash its lungs ;
   Oh, hear and grant my prayer.

TRUTHFUL BOLER'S NARROW ESCAPE.

You may talk of Georgia cyclones,
  Of Alerbamer rains—
'Bout yer South Car'liny earthquakes,
  Or Georgy harricanes;
But it's only we who've traveled
  Over the plains out west
Have ever seed th' elements
  Jest fairly do their best.

As for what you call yer cyclones
  Or harricanes yer've had,
Which brush away a town or two,
  "An' which you think so bad,
If compared to western blizzards
  In works of wreck and death,
Why, they're no more like cyclones
  Than is a baby's breath.

Of course, you've had some winters cold,
  Some summers kinder hot;
But the west can more than beat yer,
  Yet never strike a trot.
It aint no use of talkin'
  Or listenin' ter yer chumps,
Fer when it comes ter weather
  The west has got ther trumps.

14

Yer cyclones an' yer Georgy storms,
   I honestly avow,
If they occurred in Texas,
   They'd hardly stop a plow.
Unless it was in springtime,
   'Long 'bout th' fust of May,
When folks mout go er-fishing,
   Jest ter enjoy th' day.

I've seed it git so cold out thar,
   Little as yer may think,
That all the liquor 'd freeze so hard
   We couldn't git er drink,
An' ter keep ourselves from freezin'
   We'd bust th' barrel's head,
An' eat it with er knife an' fork,
   Jest like 'twas meat an' bread.

An' then I've seen it git so hot
   That every lake an' stream
Would fairly bile and cook th' fish,
   While rising fogs of steam
Would float off like er mighty cloud
   An' shet the sun from sight—
An' make the day at twelve o'clock
   As dark as at midnight.

Now, as for storms of rain an' hail,
   You fellers couldn't dream
Of sich er 'scape as I had once
   While drivin' of er team.

A six-mule perary schooner
  Ercross er Texas plain;
Oh, sich er 'scape I trust th' Lord
  I never'll have ergain.

Er hundred miles from house or tree,
  Or shed of any kind,
When all at once I seed er cloud,
  An' heard er roarin' wind,
While rain began ter fall in sheets
  At least four inches thick:
Hail, too, sot in ter comin' down
  Like walls of fallin' brick.

Th' stones were big as cocoanuts,
  Not lighter by an ounce,
An' as they hit yer oughter seed
  Jest how they'd thump and bounce.
They pounded ev'ry mule ter death,
  My wagon broke ter smash,
By time th' storm was over
  It was jest er pile of trash.

Oh, I tell yer it was awful,
  Jest almost makes me cry;
What! does any of you fellers
  S'pose I would tell er lie?
How did I escape, you ask,
  I'll tell yer all right now—
'Twas by downright darn good dodgin'
  An' by prayin'—that's jest how.

A PHILLIPIC ON EXEMPTION LAWS.

It used to be, but ain't so now, that men would pay
 their debts,
But thinking now of that time past, I sigh with vain
 regrets,
Protecting laws for scheming knaves, the bill-collector
 greets,
But nowhere in our Code we find a law against
 "dead-beats."

Exemption laws, for knaves a shield, the demagogues
 have made,
Which license gives to every thief who wills to ply
 his trade.
Our honest tradesmen vainly seek in courts their
 rights to gain,
Whilst sleek-fed rascals sit and smile to see them seek
 in vain.

Statutes of anti-garnishment, dishonest men protect,
And every poor man's word or note our tradesmen
 must reject.
For since all laws have been repealed for creditor's
 relief,
We dare not credit any man lest he should prove a
 thief.

But men with millions to invest, in goods to sell on
  time,
For poor men, spread the mortgage net and seine for
  every dime.
And they who in their meshes caught, like sheep by
  shearers' tied,
Are ofttimes clipped so close for wool, they lose
  both wool and hide.

But let us all, as honest men, these thievish laws
  efface,
They foster and encourage theft, our State they do
  disgrace.
The poor man's credit they impair, the shylock's coffers fill,
And all who advocate such laws, a prison cell should
  fill.

BOOMING BIRMINGHAM.

Now don't it beat the Juba to hear them croakers
  croak.
They seem tu think because er bank has happened tu
  git broke
That the day of judgment's cum with all its awful
  gloom,

And that Birmingham and all the world is hedding
    for the tomb ;
But I wants to tell 'em now, that in spite of all they
    say,
That Birmingham is solid, and they'd better clear the
    way.

The time is near approaching when things is gwine
    ter hum,
And we'll hear a buzz of business like bees within er
    gum ;
And every cussed croaker who wants tu save his hide
Will have ter git er hustle on or kinder stand erside,
For I feel it in my bones and breathe it in the air,
The clouds are gettin' lighter and the skies are gettin'
    fair,
The threatened storm is over and things are gettin'
    bright
And Birmingham is jest the town that's bound to
    come out right.

For she's built upon er basis of the Giberalter kind,
And she's gwine ter keep er goin' like er ship before
    the wind;
No busted bank can check her, nor nothing else can
    kill,
Tho' she's been a little crippled by that infernal bill
That keeps our honest merchants from collectin' of
    their debts,
And hobbles every workman in the commissary's
    nets.

It was made to aid the shy-locks, and was helped
    erlong by fools,
And was made intu er law by the corporation's tools.

But, Birmingham will get thar; she's er gettin' up
    her steam,
Her nozzle's pinted upward on fortune's flowing
    stream,
She's bound tu make her landing, and all who git
    aboard
Will have a glorious passage and will reap er rich re-
    ward.
And there's not a cussed croaker from Maine to
    Yubadam
Who will live tu see the sinking of our booming Bir-
    mingham.

KICKERS.

Some fokes ar born fer kickin',
　An' seem tu kick fur fun ;
Dey'll kick er man fer standin' still,
　Den kick if he should run.

Dey'll kick at ebrything dat's good,
　An' kick at what is bad ;
Dey'll kick er man fer havin' fun,
　Den kick if he gits mad.

Yer can allers find dese kickers
　At ebry place yer go,
Yer'll find dem in de meetin' house
　An' find dem at de show.

Dey are sometimes in de pulpit,
　An' sometimes in de pew ;
But yer'll allers find 'em kickin'
　At ebrything yer do.

Yer will find 'em 'bout de hotels,
　An' in de railroad trains ;
But yer'll nebber find er kicker
　Who's oberstock'd wid brains.

An' yer'll notice by obsarvin'
　A mighty sartin rule,
Dat de loudest talkin' kicker
　Am de shabbiest little fool.

An' you who's fond ob smokin'
  May put dis in yer pipe,
Dat er kicker am er greener
  Who's seldem ober-ripe.

Fer anything but kickin'
  An' fer actin' ob de fool,
An' is much mo' like er donkey
  Dan er hoss is like er mule.

An' yer cannot help concludin',
  If yer watch dese kickers right,
Dat dey's er breed ob donkeys
  Wid er gall dat's out ob sight.

An' yer'll also find by watchin'
  Anudder rule ter fit,
Dat kickers am too cowardly
  Ter face er man ob grit.

An' now befo' concludin'
  Ob what Ise had ter say,
I wants ter tell de critics
  Jest ter bray an' kick erway.

At anything dey may dislike
  Ob what dis book contains,
Fer it was'nt made tu fertilize
  Dere unproductive brains.

An' I don't care one fiddlestick
For what dese kickers say,
I've paid de printers for de job,
So let 'em kick and bray.

www.ingramcontent.com/pod-product-compliance
Lightning Source LLC
Chambersburg PA
CBHW030107030726
47498CB00007B/2286